Mayhem on the Dead River

Five Mysteries

Bill Blewett

Mayhem on the Dead River

Five Mysteries

Bill Blewett

Editors:
Barb Blewett
Katherine Kososki
Anne Nerenz

Medical Advisor: Charlene Blewett R.N.
Scenic Pictures: Peter Dishnow and Anne Nerenz

ISBN 978-0-692-68096-4

Printed in the United States of America
First Printing, 2016

Globe Printing, Inc.
200 W. Division St. Ishpeming, MI 49849
www.globeprinting.net

Dedicated to my grandchildren
Lillie, Ella, Sophie, Jack, Bryn and Ally.

Table of Contents

Part I - Murders on the Dead River 9

Part II - The Deer Trail Murders 75

Part III - Fireworks on the Dead River 141

Part IV - Winter on the Dead River 201

Part V - Revenge on the Dead River 241

Introduction:
Welcome to Victorious, Michigan

The leaves were slowly cascading down and it was quiet on the Dead River; most of the cottages were abandoned until next spring. Nearly everyone had returned to their busy lives and daily routines in the local communities.

Some Native Americans called the Dead River *Nek-omen* or *Nekominong*, which means blueberry patch of the Noque Indians. The Chippewa called it *Djibis-Manitou-Sibi*, which means river of the spirits. Sometimes a mist rises from the river like rising ghosts of departed warriors.

The Dead River is located in Mesabi County. It is in the Superior Peninsula of Michigan, near Lake Superior. Old timers talk about the thriving businesses that used to exist near its mouth. Surprisingly, entrepreneurs used to make small fortunes producing necessary goods, such as flour.

In 1889, a large sawmill was built at the mouth of the Dead River. Loggers cut at least 150,000 board feet per day during the season. A pile-driven dam was built across the mouth of the Dead River, raising the water so that the logs could be floated down to the head of the great falls. The steam hoister could lift four logs per minute out of the pond onto railroad flatcars. In 1891, 20 million board feet were cut in the saw mill and another ten million board feet were hauled to saw mills elsewhere. Dynamite was used to expedite the break-up of the ice in the spring to keep the operation going. To get the logs to the mill during a frigid January in 1896, loggers made ice roads nearly a foot thick. Single teams hauled loads up to 12,000 board feet. Such was the history of lumber on the Dead River.

Another driving force for the Superior Peninsula was iron ore, first discovered in 1844 in a nearby community called Needleton. In the 1870s, iron mining was a quarrying operation. Shafts were sunk when the surface ore was depleted and miners risked life and limb burrowing hundreds of feet underground. Eventually, steam powered machinery improved things, but it was still dirty and dangerous work.

In the 1950s, a new process was discovered for processing the estimated three and one half billion tons of ore. In 1956, near Needleton, a mill opened that crushed and separated low-grade ore from the surrounding rock. In the 1960s, another process was developed, enabling Taconite Mining to extract high-grade ore from jasper, and then melt it down, turning it into pellets. Open pit mining started near Victorious in 1974 and optimism ran high.

However, there was trouble on the horizon. New technology was decreasing the cost of production, so newer mines were opening in Minnesota. Cheap imports and automobile corporations switched to aluminum, reducing the need for steel and no longer making iron ore the best option. While the locals held out hope that the mines could continue, foreign competition would probably be the knife in the heart of both the local Mesabi County mines and the residents who called the area home, including the key characters who play important roles:

The amateur-detectives who appear in all of the stories:
- Bill Bennett, Retired Sheriff, husband to Barb
- John Baldwin, Retired Military Police Officer
- Mark Kestila, Retired Military Police Officer
- Ben Myers, Retired Victorious Police Officer
- Tyler Baldwin, Current Needleton Police Officer

Law Enforcement, who appear in nearly all of the stories
- Andy Roads, Mesabi County Sheriff's Deputy
- Carolyn Raft, Mesabi County Medical Examiner
- Strom Remington, Mesabi County Sheriff
- Officer Burns, Victorious Police Officer
- Officer Dalrymple, Needleton Police Officer

Key Dead River campers and other townsfolk who appear in one or more stories

Murder on the Dead River
- John Crane, Private Detective
- Sally and Mitch Hofsteder, Loren Luft's neighbors
- Loren Luft, Ronnie McCann's brother
- Denny Marsh, pool shark and Needleton thug
- Nancy Mather, widowed sister to Loren Luft and Ronnie McCann, mother of four young children
- Ronnie McCann, Loren Luft's sister and receptionist at the local car dealership
- Gary Payne, the best golfer at Gitchigoomie Golf Course
- Scott Randall, a salesman at the local car dealership
- Carl Swanson, attorney
- Don Dempster, Mesabi County Employee
- Connie Timmerman, Tom Timmerman's ex-wife
- Tom Timmerman, *Rocky's Bar* Owner

The Deer Trail Murders
- Cindy Mason, WQPF news reporter
- Debbie Kinsely, WQPF receptionist
- Jack Cannon, WQPF sports reporter
- Lana Kanton, WQPF weather forecaster
- Pete Cotter, WQPF manager

Fireworks on the Dead River
- Jim, Janet, and Kelly Sanderson
- Ken, Betty, and Jenni Durant
- Ace Wilson
- Larry Fender
- Clare Helmon, Larry Fender's sister
- Clyde Helmon, Clare Helmon's husband
- Jack Storm
- Mother Storm-Larry's and Clare's Mother
- Valerie Baldwin, John Baldwin's Wife

Winter on the Dead River
- Craig Raft, Carolyn Raft's former husband

Part I

Murders on the Dead River

Chapter One

My wife, Barb, and I have lived our entire lives in Victorious. From our home, we can see the open pit mine a few miles away. On a quiet day, we can even hear the four hundred ton capacity trucks hauling iron ore up the mile-long grade to the top of the pit, only to return back down empty, reload, and creep their way back up again.

As the snow melts and the weather improves, we move out to the Dead River. We love living in Victorious, but the summers on the Dead River are special. It is exciting to become reacquainted with our neighbors again. There are almost four hundred families who own a parcel of land along the Dead River. Everyone is very protective of his or her property lines. Rumors run rampant: One landowner even went out in the dead of winter to move the metal lot line markers to gain additional access to the river. In the spring, a disagreement broke out that would rival the Hatfield's and McCoy's.

My name is Bill Bennett. I am a retired sheriff. I had spent thirty-three years as a law enforcement officer. The last twelve were as sheriff of Mesabi County, which is located in the heart of the Superior Peninsula. Barb, my wife, had just retired, from a teaching career at Victorious High School.

Everything was perfect. We just didn't know what was coming.

Saturday

The day started like any other day. Barb had just finished her four-mile run out to our mailbox and back. I was waiting on the deck with a hot cup of java for both of us. Just then, a sheriff's cruiser pulled up. I recognized the sheriff's deputy, Andy Roads. He stepped out of his cruiser, shaking hands. "How's retirement treating you?" Andy asked.

"Great! I'm enjoying it more every day. You'll have to bring your fishing pole next time," I replied.

"I will. Right now, though, I'm on official business. Did you hear anything unusual last night?"

Barb and I looked at each other and said, "No, what happened?"

"Ronnie McCann was raped and murdered last night. Are you sure you didn't hear something?"

"No, I'm so sorry, but we didn't," I said.

"I can't believe that could happen here," Barb said.

"Have you checked with any of the other neighbors?" I asked.

"So far we haven't had any luck," Deputy Roads replied.

"If you think of something, give us a call," Deputy Roads said.

Andy Roads stepped back into his cruiser, driving away.

Apparently, it had all started several months earlier. Her name was Ronalyn McCann. She was known as Ronnie to her friends. She was twenty-five. Her long brown hair and curvaceous body made her a true looker. She worked as a receptionist at a local car dealership. She possessed a friendly demeanor. One man who read too much into her sweetness was a salesman named Scott Randall. He believed that they might be able to become more than acquaintances, although she never encouraged him.

She had moved back from Midland to stay with her brother, Loren Luft, on the Dead River. She wanted a trial separation from her husband, Tom McCann. Apparently, Ronnie's husband decided he wanted his freedom after only two years of matrimony. The separation was messy, leaving hard feelings. She wanted to be with family.

To compound the problem, Loren's and Ronnie's sister, Nancy Mather, and her four children had moved in with Loren, too. Her husband had recently died from a short, but horrific fight with pancreatic cancer. The children were dealing with the loss of their dad as well as could be expected, and Nancy felt that they needed a man in their life, so she had asked Loren if they could stay for a while until she got on her feet. Truth be told, she also needed a shoulder to lean on.

When Ronnie's car needed repairs, Scott Randall was happy to pick her up in the morning and chauffer her to work. When he dropped Ronnie off at her brother's at night, Scott would come in for a drink. He and Loren would talk about their latest rounds of golf, which conveniently allowed plenty of time for Scott to cast his eyes on Ronnie. Just seeing her was enough for him. Every weekend, he would make it a point to happen by while she was enjoying the sun's rays outside, although with her sister Nancy, her brother Loren, and her three nieces and her nephew, there wasn't much time for private talk.

Scott also put together a golf outing every Monday night at Gitchigoomie Golf Course, a tough eighteen-hole course with a good reputation. The course was built in the late 19th century by Taconite mining executives. Rumor had it that Gerald Ford played it once in the early 1970s. Scott always invited Loren and their friends Ben Myers and Mark Kestila to make up a foursome, thinking that working his way into Loren's good graces would help win Ronnie's affection.

The best golfer at Gitchigoomie was Gary Payne. When he was young, he had lived in the fast lane, loving fast cars and faster women. Eventually, he grew tired of the free-swinging life and settled down, marrying a beautiful girl from Victorious. With his playboy days over, he was content to earn a moderate salary selling tires to the Taconite Iron Mine and taking money from middle-aged duffers at Gitchigoomie. Many times, Gary Payne would even give them a few stroke lead just to see if he could still win money from each of them. He knew how to draw a shot and make putts. Many opponents challenged him, but he won every time. You could usually tell whom he had been playing as they would storm into the bar, demanding their favorite drink. Gary Payne wasn't lucky; he was good, but he had a drinking problem, although his wife, Jenny, stuck by him over the years. She was just plain tough. Gary Payne was the ultimate good-time Charley, he made sure he bought the Taconite mine executives ample drinks, so that they would remember him when it came time to purchase new tires. Whenever anyone had tried to get him to join AA, he refused to listen; however, in August the previous year, Gary had a near miss that could have been catastrophic: he had passed out at the wheel, crossing the center line, narrowly missing a car with a mom and her two children. Gary raced to their minivan. "I'm sorry. Are you okay?" he asked.

"I think we are," said the mother, visibly trembling, she said, "You could have killed us."

"My name is Gary Payne. Let me know if there is anything I can do," he said.

She nodded, driving away at a very slow speed. He experienced an epiphany. You usually don't get a second chance. As I drove into Victorious that Wednesday night, I passed St. James' Church and saw Gary going into the AA meeting. I smiled.

Chapter Two

The lot west of Loren Luft's had been recently purchased by a professional couple, Milt and Sally Hofsteder. They wanted to build their dream home. It was a multi-level, six thousand square foot home with a beautiful view overlooking the river. However, to do so, they would need every inch of property. The Campers Club, whose president was Dan Sundell, controlled all property construction. They stipulated that structures could not be closer than ten feet from the property line.

The Hofsteders had asked for a variance to the rule. Loren had argued against the variance at a hearing in August and the request was denied. Needless to say, there were harsh words exchanged between the neighbors during the next few months. Although Ronnie McCann was not involved, she couldn't help feeling uneasy as the Hofsteders glared at her when both families happened to be on the beach at the same time. As fall set in, the Hofsteders continued to press Ronnie McCann's brother Loren to drop his opposition to the variance and change his vote. He refused. When, with the first frost, the leaves started to turn color, it became apparent that construction wasn't going to start that year. Soon the snow would come and any construction would have to be postponed until spring. The Hofsteders were desperate; they had to change Loren's opposition to the variance.

They retained an attorney, Carl Swanson, who was a partner in a prestigious law firm, *Preston and Swanson*. The hiring was no accident – Swanson also lived on the Dead River, a few miles upstream. Although Carl lobbied Ronnie's brother relentlessly with arguments in favor of the variance, saying it would increase everyone's property value if the home could be built, Loren refused to budge.

The Hofsteders next approached an individual who had connections with some seedy characters. His name was Denny Marsh. He was tall and broad shouldered, standing all of six foot five inches. He had black steely eyes that could look right through you. Marsh was not above using tough tactics: individuals who had gotten in Marsh's way had been beaten up. Others had to swerve off the road to avoid an accident. The Hofsteders clearly were desperate.

Hofsteder had heard that Denny Marsh hung around *Rocky's Bar* in Needleton. He decided to pay him a visit, entering the bar, and asking the bartender which one was Marsh.

"He's the big one racking up the pool balls."

Hofsteder stepped toward Marsh.

"Are you Denny Marsh?" Hofsteder asked.

Marsh nodded his head.

"Could I see you for a minute? I have a prospective job for you." Marsh put his cue stick down, leading Hofsteder to a table.

"Who's asking?" Marsh asked.

"I'm Milt Hofsteder. I want to hire you to persuade someone to give me a variance on our property. We have a problem with the neighbor."

"It'll cost you five thousand dollars up front and another five thousand when the job is done," Marsh sneered.

"That's fine. I just want the variance by next spring. Can you do it?"

"Who do you want me to persuade?"

"Loren Luft – he lives next to me on the Dead River. I don't want him hurt. I just want to scare him."

"I'll see what I can do. I want the cash by tomorrow night," Marsh said.

"I can do that," Milt Hofsteder said. Smiling contentedly at the thought that he actually might get his beloved variance, Hofsteder turned and left, although he breathed a sigh of relief when stepping outside into the fresh air. He wasn't used to dealing with guys who didn't play by the rules.

In spite of some threatening phone calls and slashed tires

over the next week, Loren Luft still refused to renege on his opposition to the variance.

Back at the car dealership, Scott Randall was getting nowhere with Ronnie McCann, as hard as he tried to work his way in to her good graces. He was running out of options and he knew he had to do something to change her attitude and attract her attention. His sure-fire plan was winning the sales competition that month at the dealership – First prize was an all-expense paid trip to Las Vegas for the salesman and a guest. She would surely want to go to Las Vegas with him. Of course he would promise it was purely platonic.

Scott stayed late every night for a week planning his strategy. He decided he would go through the phone book contacting every potential business. Then, when the new month arrived, he started making calls. At first, nobody was interested. Gradually, he was able to persuade a few plumbing businesses to replace their aging vans. He even persuaded a health care company to order a new fleet of vehicles. Finally, he was able to secure an order of three moving vans from the Victorious Moving Company. This last order put him over the top. Nobody else was even close. By the end of the month, he was assured of victory, and hopefully, Ronnie's affection.

As he approached her with the ticket vouchers in his pocket, he could hardly contain his desire. Scott asked, "Say, Ronnie! Would you like to accompany me to Las Vegas? I think it would be fun."

"No thanks, I really don't like the fast pace, but thanks for asking. I appreciate it," she said. His anger bubbled over. He could barely control himself. He stormed out of the dealership, walking around to the back of the building where he promptly kicked the dumpster with disgust. He had worked so hard to win the competition and the accompanying foregone conclusion of Ronnie's affection. Now the trip meant nothing to him. If he could not take Ronnie with him, there was no point in even going. Scott Randall was desperate to persuade her somehow to change her mind.

Meanwhile, after two months of surreal independence, Ronnie's estranged husband, Tom McCann, realized his life was not what he had hoped. Bar hopping and womanizing wasn't what he thought it would be. Waking up on bar floors, or in strange hotel rooms, was not what he imagined when he left Victorious for the big cities in Lower Michigan. He had plenty of sex, even a few heated romantic flings. They were short lived, leaving him empty. He had lost his job as a cable lineman due to his excessive absenteeism and two DUI's. He had hit rock bottom.

With no job, no romantic interests, and no reason for staying, McCann decided to return to Mesabi County. It was time to pursue Ronnie again. He could change. He'd had his fling with independence, but it wasn't worth it. He would have to find her and win her back. Surely, he could do it one more time. Tom McCann loaded his black Ford pick-up truck and headed north.

Chapter Three

In Victorious, my neighbor, Mark Kestila and I were long time friends. After high school, he had enlisted in the Army and was sent to Europe, where he served as an undercover officer in the bars. When his tour was over, he was glad to come home to the Superior Peninsula to enjoy our quality of life. We had duck hunted together for many years, usually coming back with our limit. There was no shortage of good times and funny stories. Now that we were both retired, we'd just meet for a cup of coffee at *Millie's*, a local diner, and allow the ducks to fly south for the winter. It was a win-win for everyone, man and beast alike.

Another good friend, Ben Meyers, was a retired police officer from Victorious. His detective skills were exceptional, which is a good thing because he was responsible for uncovering the drug manufacturers and distributors in Victorious. To say Ben Myers was tenacious would be an understatement. He and the city got a bad rap for being the home for a lot of drug dealing. Now retired, Ben enjoyed fishing and playing golf.

Upon hearing of the rape and murder the previous night, Mark and Ben drove out to the Dead River to peruse the crime scene. Ben was allowed entry because of his former status in the Victorious Police Department. He learned the rudimentary aspects of the crime: When Ronnie failed to come to breakfast after repeated calls, Nancy opened Ronnie's bedroom door and saw the horrific scene. They all realized that the crime must have taken place while the rest of the family was at a wedding reception in Victorious the previous night.

After discussing the available details with Mark, who had waited in the car, they drove over to my place, which was just a few doors down. I was a little surprised to see a second vehicle approach right after Deputy Roads had departed. Ben could not divulge anything, of course, that might interfere with the case, so I knew enough not to ask prying questions, even though my curiosity was getting the better of me.

"Hello, Bill," Ben said.

"Hello, how are you?" I asked.

"Good," Ben said.

"Did you hear anything last night?" Ben asked.

"No, Deputy Roads just left after asking me the same question. Unfortunately, we didn't hear a thing," I said.

"It's hard to imagine something like that happening on the Dead River," Ben said.

"Yes, I know, that was terrible. I wish I could have helped. I feel terrible for her and her family," I said.

"Whoever attacked Ronnie must be one sick son-of-a-bitch," Mark said.

I said, "I agree. I have seen a lot of rotten things in my life, but that's one of the worst."

"We'll have to see what happens," Ben said.

"Take care," he said, as he drove away.

Two days passed and no arrests were made. Curiosity continued to eat at me. I ventured over to the sheriff's office on Monday morning, experiencing *déjà vu* as I entered the office and exchanged pleasantries with the office personnel and the deputies on duty. It felt strange to enter my old office and see my former under-sheriff's name on the door. But, Strom Remington was a good man and I had supported him in the last election.

He said, "It appeared Ronnie's killer slipped away into the night... no DNA, just a key chain with a golf club emblem on it."

"Do you have a suspect?" I asked.

"That's just it, there are no lack of suspects. At the top of the list is her estranged husband, Tom McCann. He just returned to Victorious and is renting a room at the Moonlight Motel. No credible alibi – he said he was watching television that evening and only left to get a meal at the nearby McDonald's. Neither the drive-by cashier, nor the food dispenser could recall if anyone fitting his description had driven through and the security camera wasn't even working. A camera at a near-by bank did record a black Ford pick-up truck driving in that direction at the corresponding time, but it was too far to see the license plate clearly," Sheriff Remington said.

He continued, "Then there's Denny Marsh ... he has an alibi, but it's shaky at best. Supposedly, he had been shooting pool at *Rocky's*. Many patrons swore he was there the entire night, even running the table once, although their credibility is questionable; for now his alibi is holding."

"Huh. Denny Marsh' friends would alibi for him in a heartbeat," I said.

"Milt Hofsteder claimed he was home the entire evening. Sally Hofsteder vouched for him, saying they had rented some movies. After a call to their previous residence and from inquiring about their background, it seems Sally met Milt and fell in love with his money and the lifestyle he could provide. The chief of police also felt that Milt possessed a quick temper and a demanding personality," Remington said.

"I wonder how they ended up here," I said.

Sheriff Remington said, "Milt rose quickly in the business world, from a basic chemistry tech into higher and higher management positions, stepping on anyone who got in his way. He's the CEO of Pearl, Inc. Now, it's the nickel mining company that's just getting started north of the Dead River. Milt is used to getting his way and is not the kind of man who takes "No" for an answer." Sheriff Remington continued, "Carl Swanson, who was retained as the Luft's attorney, is out of town."

"I think it might be worth looking into whether or not he was on that flight," I said.

He cannot be reached for a week. His paralegal, Sandy Sundell, will contact us when he returns. When pressed regarding his whereabouts on that Saturday, she told me he had taken the 1:00 flight to California. He flew out of Mesabi International Airport; he couldn't have been involved," Sheriff Remington said.

The sheriff said, "That leaves just one suspect, Scott Randall."

"The car salesman?" I asked.

"Yes. Nobody has heard from him in over a week. His office manager told my deputies he had started acting erratic. He even turned down the first-prize Las Vegas trip that he won the previous month. After refusing the trip, he asked for a week off. I feel Scott Randall is the number one suspect."

I left the sheriff's office with more questions than when I entered. Was Carl Swanson actually on that flight? Could Milt Hofsteder be involved? How did the perpetrator get away? If he, or she, had driven a vehicle over to Luft's home, why hadn't someone seen it? It was Friday night and there was a lot of traffic on that road. If the attacker had arrived by boat, someone certainly would have heard, or seen it – there were a lot of people enjoying campfires on the shore that night, and someone should have spotted a boat leaving a dock at midnight. Why would anyone want to hurt that young woman? What was the reason for the crime?

Chapter Four

I returned to our cottage to ponder the dilemma on our deck with a cold beverage. It just seemed ideas flowed better with a cold one in hand. Inspiration struck: I called my good friend, John Baldwin, twenty-year military police officer who had ten years' detective work in the Air Force. We had been boyhood friends. After high school, I chose law enforcement while he joined and proceeded to rise quickly through the ranks in the military police. John's son, Tyler, was also a veteran, from Desert Storm. He was currently an officer on the Needleton Police Force and would be a great asset to our team.

We decided to gather the team that night at *Geno's Pizzeria*, home of the best pizza and the coldest beer. The owner was Rick Bonnetelli. He was the proprietor of the popular restaurant that had been handed down from father to son for over seventy years. A wiry man in his mid-fifties, he wore a big grin, had a kind disposition, and liked to do juggling tricks for children when they came in with their parents.

After a few pitchers were downed and ample pizza had been consumed, the team – Mark, Ben, John, Tyler and I got down to the task at hand.

"We have to uncover how someone could have gotten away unnoticed," I said.

"Mark and I will canvass the south side of the Dead River, checking with the campers," Ben said.

"Tyler and I can investigate the opposite side, hoping someone saw something," John said.

"Since I live nearby, I said, I will go back to Loren Luft's cottage, where Ronnie was living, in hopes that her brother, or other family members might have left out some details," I said.

Chapter Five

Wednesday morning
As I approached the Luft's cottage, I noticed that the door was ajar. I knocked and the door swung open. I called for Loren, then for his sister Nancy, but nobody answered. The television was on, and a moaning sound was coming from the back bedroom. I stepped in and was instantly knocked semi-conscious, then dragged by the feet to the river. I felt cold water rushing over my face, into my lungs, over my head. I struggled, but it was useless.

The Dead is famous for having a strong current, and I was caught and swept down steam, unable to help myself. Barely keeping my head above water, I drifted with the current until I finally recognized a familiar cove. Feebly kicking my way toward the shore, I must have made enough of a splash that John Baldwin saw me. He dove into the river, grabbed my jacket, and dragged me to shore. His son, Tyler, arrived and together they helped me to my feet. I had no idea what had happened. John asked, "How do you feel and what were you doing in the river?"

I said, "I feel terrible and I'm not sure what happened. I went to Loren's cottage; the door was ajar and I heard moaning from one of the back bedrooms. Then someone hit me from behind, dragged me to the water, throwing me in." As my head started to clear, the three of us drove back upstream to the Luft cottage.

As we entered, we could still hear the television, but the moaning had stopped. We carefully looked in each room, making our way to the back bedroom. There on the floor was Ronnie's sister, Nancy Mather. From the bruises on her neck, it appeared she had been strangled, but that was for the M.E. to determine. Tyler whipped out his phone and called 911.

It seemed like an eternity for the emergency vehicles to arrive. Finally, the sheriff's deputy, Andy Roads, pulled up. The paramedics arrived a few minutes later, but they could not revive her. Deputy Roads took down the story, from our five-man sleuthing plan to the assault on me. Neighbors were gathering. Everyone wanted to know what had happened. Feeling guilty I wondered aloud if I could have saved her if I had been five minutes earlier.

"Maybe, yes, and maybe you'd be dead," John said matter-of-factly.

I nodded, thinking that my brush with death would become the stuff that nightmares are made of for a long while.

When Loren Luft arrived on the scene, he was beside himself. Upon entering the cottage, hearing the news, he fell to his knees, sobbing uncontrollably. He held the family picture of the three of them as children – Loren in the middle; Nancy on the right; Ronnie on the left – to his chest crying, "*Why, Why?*" Nobody had an answer.

Wednesday afternoon

Mark and Ben finally had some good news: "In canvassing door–to–door, they dropped in on Kenny and Megan Bievins' cottage around the bend. They had been out on their pontoon boat during the evening of the first murder," Mark said.

"Why didn't they come forward earlier?" I asked.

Ben said, "They were downstate when the murder occurred, visiting his sister; they only heard about it when they returned. The Bievins said that they took a midnight cruise the night of the murder and saw a kayak, surprised that anyone else was out as late as they were."

"Did they see who was in it?" I asked.

Ben said, "No, it was quite far away."

We returned to my cottage and navigated up and down the Dead River for hours in my pontoon boat, hoping we could find the kayak. No luck. If it weren't for bad luck, we would have had none at all, but the five of us agreed not to give up. We owed it to the two women. As we tied the pontoon to my dock, we discussed the case.

"If we can find evidence for one murder, we might solve both," I said.

"The question that keeps haunting me is why did the murderer return and kill Nancy," Ben asked.

"What could she have known that she had to be eliminated?" Mark asked.

"Did she know something that she had kept to herself?" I asked.

"If she did, she took the secret to the grave," Tyler Baldwin stated.

"Tyler and I will pay a visit to Tom McCann. Maybe, we could shake some information out of him," John said.

Later that day they drove to the Moonlight Motel in Victorious, entered the office and asked the owners, "What room is Tom McCann's?"

"You know we can't tell you that, but he usually leaves early in the morning and he doesn't return until late at night. I think he likes to gamble. He usually tells us if he wins. He just left an hour ago," the owner said.

The closest casino was in Choctaw Township, about an hour away. Since Tom had apparently just left, John and Tyler decided they had time to see if McCann had any incriminating evidence in his room. Only one room had the door closed – the rest were open for cleaning. It was pretty apparent which one he occupied. It was an older motel, with dead bolt locks. After jiggling his credit card, John was able to slide the dead bolt inward and, once inside, they knew where to look. Tyler lifted the top of the toilet to see if McCann had drugs. There was marijuana in a plastic bag; he slid the lid back on the toilet. After checking under the mattress and coming up empty, they pulled out the top dresser drawer. Behind it were divorce papers signed by Ronnie, but not signed by Tom. Apparently, he'd had second thoughts about his search for a perfect life with another woman.

They returned everything as it had been, but as they were leaving, they heard a car door slam followed by the beep of a car lock. They had to act fast. They scurried into the bathroom, climbed into the shower, and closed the curtain behind them. They heard the motel room door open and close. The television was turned on and a sigh of relief was heard as McCann fell on the bed. It wasn't long before they heard snoring. Slowly, they drew the curtain open, removed their shoes, and slid past the snoring McCann. They slowly opened the door. The hinges made the customary squeak, but McCann didn't budge. They left and carefully closed the door behind them. McCann pulled the covers off, drew the curtain back, and watched them drive away with a wry smile on his face.

As they were pulling out of the hotel parking lot, John looked at his watch. It was approaching 3:00. "We might be able to golf at Gitchigoomie," he said.

"That sounds like a possibility. We probably could get eighteen in; loser buys dinner," said Tyler, never one to pass up a good challenge.

"I think you beat me by five strokes last time. Maybe a handicap should be in order. What do you say you spot me a stroke on the first five holes?" John said coyly. He had to set the trap just right, or his son wouldn't bite.

"I don't think so. I am not falling for that old trick. We play straight up," Tyler said.

"What about dropping the worst score from the card?"

"I can live with that," Tyler said. "Prepare to be destroyed. Remember that we putt everything in. No gimmes. No matter how close they are. Loser buys dinner."

It goes without saying, they were unavailable for the remainder of the day.

Chapter Six

Friday afternoon

Ronnie McCann's and Nancy Luft's joint funeral was beautiful, but afterward, at home, reality was setting in. The post-funeral crowd had come and gone. It seemed like the entire Campers' Club, except for the Hofsteders, had come both to the church and to Luft's house afterward. On the counter, food piled up, but nobody was thinking about eating. In the kitchen, Barb was washing the dishes and Dorothy Harris was wiping them as fast as Barb could hand them to her.

Nancy's four children sat forlorn through the hugs and pinching of cheeks. Nikki and Luke didn't understand why everyone cried when they made eye contact. It was easier to just stare at the floor. None of them felt like eating – their mommy wasn't there to fix their plates, encouraging them to eat. She knew how to get them to eat. That was gone now.

Father Don shook everyone's hand before he left and whispered, "So sad; it's so sad." Many of us remained in the living room making small talk, trying to predict what was going to happen to the children. We all agreed Loren was a nice guy and would do right by them, but it would never be the same.

After a while, the children shuffled off into their bedroom, sitting on their beds and just looking at their feet. Katie, the oldest at ten, was in no mood to play. Anna, the serious one at eight years old, didn't even look at her Barbie dolls. Nikki, age six, was the theatrical one. Luke, age four, didn't really understand anything that was going on. As the crowd thinned, then disappeared completely, Uncle Loren came into their bedroom; he sat with them on the edge of the bed, patting Nikki's and Luke's backs. He looked at each of them individually, but didn't know what to say. They sat in silence. Finally, Uncle Loren said, "You can stay here with me as long as you want. We're a family."

Why couldn't things go back to the way they were? They had been a family before, with a mom and a dad. Now both of their parents were gone forever. Katie and Anna threw their dolls and stuffed animals to the floor, bursting into tears. Nikki and Luke started crying, too. Uncle Loren said, "Mommy's in heaven now and she is watching over you."

"We want her here," Nikki said.

"I fell down yesterday, skinning my knee. She wasn't here to kiss it, making it better," Luke said.

"We miss the way she used to put whipped cream on our pancakes," Katie said.

"When she was done, she would put a dot of whipped cream on our noses," Anna said.

"Who's going to help pick out our clothes? Katie asked.

"I will help you," Loren said.

"You're not Mommy," Anna said, starting to cry.

"Who's going to read a bedtime story to me?" Luke asked.

"I will read it to you every night. I promise," Loren said.

"Who's going to comb our hair? Nobody could do it like she could. She brushed it until it was just right. She used to put a barrette in my hair when she was finished," Nikki said.

"She always washed my Batman shirt every night. Now what will I wear?" Luke asked.

"I'll wash it every night," Loren said, fighting back tears.

Loren put his arms around all of them, hugging them. They cried together. Life was unexplainable sometimes.

Stepping outside, the sun was still shining and a warm breeze was blowing off the river. Two eagles flew overhead looking majestic as always. They just glided along, occasionally, flapping their wings ever so slightly. It was almost as if Nancy and Ronnie were looking down from heaven, saying good-bye.

"Do you think we should go over and mess with Hofsteder a little?" John asked.

"What about McCann? I have my suspicions about him," Mark added.

"Personally, I would like a word with that attorney Swanson just for old times' sake. He once helped get a drug dealer off on a technicality," Tyler said. "And Scott Randall has some explaining to do, too."

"No, I think it's been a long day. We'll get a fresh start tomorrow. There is no lack of suspects, that's for certain," I said, but no one moved. Somehow, it seemed that, if we stood there in silence staring at the river, things would improve; we knew better. For the first time, the river didn't look so beautiful. As tough as we thought we were, we all felt empty. Even Ben wiped his eyes.

Back in the house, the two younger children needed to move, so Anna suggested indoor hide-and-seek the way they use to play it with Mommy. Uncle Loren and Katie begrudgingly agreed. Nikki and Luke smiled for the first time in days, then ran and hid in their favorite place, the back of Mommy's closet. After counting to ten, Uncle Loren, Katie and Anna started slowly after them. After the usual round of loud and mystified poor guesses about where the children were hiding, Luke couldn't wait inside the closet any longer and simply stepped out from behind the door. Anna noticed something sticky on Luke's leg, maybe grease from the closet door hinges, or perhaps dried jelly, or frosting from the post-funeral desserts? Uncle Loren took Luke into the bathroom to clean him up. Nobody knew what that would lead to.

Chapter Seven

Friday evening

Next door, Sally Hofsteder couldn't stand it anymore. She had gone days without sleeping and hoped for a nap in the Adirondack chair on the front porch. She was still hoping for that nap when the sun went down and when it came up again the next morning. She had tried to talk to her husband, but he only pushed her away. She simply had to turn to the only man she could really trust, Carl Swanson.

After arriving in California, Carl Swanson couldn't believe his good fortune. He had purchased a package to play the best golf courses and his paralegal, Sandy Sundell, had booked him into five top courses in the area, from Pebble Beach to Torrey Pines. On the trip back to Victorious, he was feeling pretty good about himself.

The plane touched down at Mesabi International Airport. He deplaned and waited for his suitcase and golf clubs. By the time he had his clubs; most of the terminal was empty. As he turned from the luggage carousel, there stood Sally Hofsteder. She approached him and gave him a welcome-home hug that suggested that they were more than just friends.

"How was your flight? I missed you," Sally said.

"Sandy Sundell told me what happened to Nancy Mather and about the double funeral," Carl said.

She took his suitcase and they held hands as they made their way out of the airport.

Saturday morning

If there was a more serene sight in the world, I had never seen it. Fishermen were slowly making their way east toward the dam – the weeds around the mouth of the tributaries made this area a prime spot to reel in bass or northern pike. I was enjoying Mother Nature at her finest and Barb was making her daily run to the mailboxes. When a vehicle pulled into the driveway, I knew they had come to see me. It was Loren. Approaching me with a look of determination, he demanded to know if I had heard anything.

"I have been to the state police and the sheriff's department already and they won't tell me a thing about my sisters' deaths," Loren lamented.

"No, I haven't heard anything yet. It's only been a few days," I said.

"I know, but I'm going crazy and I have my suspicions; if the law doesn't make an arrest soon, I'm going to take care of it myself.'"

"That's the last thing you should be thinking about," I said. "Go home and take care of your nieces and nephew. They lost their dad and now they've lost their mother. They need you more than ever."

"Someone's going to pay and I have a good idea who is responsible," Loren bellowed as he got back into his car and sped away.

Barb returned with a bewildered look on her face just as the dust was beginning to settle. "Who was that? He almost hit me," she uttered.

"Loren Luft. Of course, he is having a difficult time. I guess I would feel the same way. He is extremely frustrated with the lack of progress in the case," I said.

I handed her a cup of coffee, and we proceeded to the deck to watch the morning unfold.

At about the same time of day, Milt Hofsteder decided to encourage Denny March to complete the job he was being paid for. Hofsteder stepped into *Rocky's, Denny* Marsh's favorite waterhole, and needed more than a few minutes for his eyes to adjust to the extremely dim light inside. The usual barflies one could find at any gin joint in the country were staring straight ahead, hoping somehow their lives could improve all on their own. Hofsteder heard the crack of pool balls striking one another on the other side of the bar and approached Marsh with caution. "You called this meeting. What do you want?" Denny Marsh snarled.

"I was hoping you could give me some news regarding the variance for the property line."

"Are you nuts? The heat is on, and until they find out who killed those two women, nothing is going to happen. Now get out and don't call me again. Do you hear?" Marsh said menacingly, staring right at Hofsteder.

"But I paid you five thousand dollars to do a job and I expect you to do it," whispered Hofsteder. He backed up, feeling safer, and left quickly. Nobody at the bar even looked his way, for fear they might spill a drop of their courage. Hofsteder was not used to dealing with people like this, and decided then and there that he would have to find another way to get the variance.

When Milt Hofsteder returned home, his wife Sally seemed a little calmer than when he last saw her. They made small talk, then eating their meal in silence, as was their custom.

Sally went out to the deck to sit in the Adirondack to wait for the sunset. Instead of joining her, Milt took out his house plans, scrutinizing them on the kitchen table. How could he get the variance now with all that had happened, particularly since his henchman had failed to do anything at all? There was only one thing to do.

Monday morning a sheepish Scott Randall walked through the showroom doors. He stared sadly at Ronnie McCann's empty desk, then walked over to his own desk and sat down. A few of the other salesmen nodded, but several just ignored him. No one knew what to say. Seeing Scott at his regular desk about to resume business as usual, the manager, Les Condo, called him into his office. "How are you doing Scott?" he asked. "Have a seat."

"I'm doing okay, I guess."

"With everything going on, do you need more time off? The police have been here asking about you. Have they caught up with you yet?" Condo asked.

"No, they haven't."

"Well, for the good of the company, I think you should take some time off. We'll call you back, if and when we need you. I hope you understand," Les Condo stated.

Scott Randall stood up and, without even looking at Condo, or the other sales staff, walked out of the showroom

Chapter Eight

Tuesday evening

It was time for another meeting at *Geno's Pizzeria*. When we arrived, Rick Bonnetelli was behind the bar as usual; he greeted the five of us with a sympathetic smile. We ordered several pizzas and pitchers of beer. I will tell you right now that you wouldn't want to get between this crew and their beer and pizza. Afterward, we got down to business. John and Tyler brought us up to speed on their investigation of Tom McCann's motel room. The fact that he hadn't signed the divorce papers only convinced us that he didn't want one anymore.

"He may have attacked Ronnie McCann in a fit of rage when he found he couldn't have her back," John said.

"But why would he kill Nancy Mather a few days later?" Mark argued.

"Loren drove to my cottage yesterday, making threats that he was going to take the law into his own hands if something didn't break," I said. "I tried to calm him down, telling him we were working the case along with the sheriff and state police. What do you have to report, Tyler?"

Tyler stated, "I called Mesabi International Airport. It appears that Swanson really was on the 1:00 flight to California—one of the baggage handlers saw him actually get on the plane."

"According to Sheriff Remington, both Carl Swanson and Scott Randall are back in town. It should be easy to track them down and check their whereabouts when Nancy was murdered," Ben said. "We can also verify a few things about where they were when Ronnie was killed, too."

"Tyler and I can follow Scott Randall," John said

"Mark and I can follow Carl Swanson," Ben said.

We adjourned. Hopefully, we would catch a break in at least one of the cases.

Desperately wanting to find his sisters' killer – or maybe there were two of them out there – Loren went on the internet and searched for private detectives who would be willing to travel and qualified to deal with this kind of situation. And it didn't take long to find one. His name was John Crane, a former Green Beret and a veteran of the Iraqi War. Crane had served as a guard at Guantanamo Bay, been wounded twice, awarded the Bronze Star as well as the Purple Heart and was trained in martial arts and an assortment of other deadly weapons.

John Crane wouldn't come cheap: in his e-mail response, Crane made it clear that his price was one hundred thousand dollars up front and another one hundred thousand dollars after the case was closed. He would be on a plane to Mesabi International Airport as soon as possible and would let Loren know when to pick him up.

Wednesday morning

As one passenger after another deplaned at the Mesabi International airport, Luft saw a giant come through the door wearing army fatigues, unshaven, about six foot–two inches tall and weighing a chiseled two hundred and fifty pounds.

"Are you John Crane?" Loren asked.

Crane nodded and said, "Who's asking?"

"I'm Loren Luft. We have a deal. Can you find out who murdered my sisters?"

John Crane said, "Yes, but I need the details."

"Nearly everyone in our family went to a wedding reception last Friday night, but my sister Ronnie stayed home. I begged her to come, but she said she was tired. While she was sleeping, someone broke in through Ronnie's bedroom window, beat, raped, and then murdered her."

"Not a random attack. Who was so enraged with her that he'd beat her to death?" Crane asked.

"I'm not sure. My sister Nancy found her the next day. Then six days later, someone broke in again, strangling her, too. I lost two sisters in six days," Luft said.

"Did Ronnie have any troubles, or have you had issues with anyone?"

"Not sure about Ronnie; there's a former car salesman who used to hang around making small talk with me just to catch sight of her. No one would hurt Nancy; she was nice to everyone. As for me, I've got a problem with my neighbor, Milt Hofsteder. He wants to construct a mega-house right on our property line and I won't agree. First, he hired a lawyer, Carl Swanson, to help me change my mind. And rumor has it he also hired a thug named Denny Marsh to intimidate me; I've had my tires slashed and have received threatening phone calls, but no personal attacks."

"I'll check out Marsh and get back to you. Right now, I need a shower and some sleep. Take me to the nearest hotel." Crane took out a cigarette and lit it. After exhaling, he looked at Loren, "I should be able to find the murderer. Do you want me to just kill whoever is responsible?"

"No, just call me with the info and I'll do the rest," Luft said.

Crane said, "OK, but remember, you are not to ask any questions and under no circumstances are you to contact me. After I find the murderer, you will transfer the one hundred thousand dollar balance to my account."

Loren agreed, wondering if he had done the right thing.

Earlier that same morning, I was driving to Loren's house hoping to reassure him that everyone was doing everything they could to find the killers. As I was approaching his house, he cruised by me as though I were invisible. I did a slow U-turn, following him, wondering where he could be going so early in the morning. To my chagrin, he drove to the airport. I decided to hang around and see if he was leaving, or waiting to meet someone. When he walked out with a chiseled Man-Mountain, I couldn't imagine what he was up to, but my sixth sense kicked in and decided I had better follow along to see what was afoot.

Sticking just close enough to see what was happening, I watched Loren Luft drop the Man-Mountain off at the Holiday Inn. There were no good-byes. It actually appeared that the behemoth gave Loren the creeps.

After Luft drove off, I parked, slipped nonchalantly into the hotel lobby, saw Man-Mountain walking to the elevator and quickly followed, feeling small standing next to him in the elevator. He stepped off on the second floor; I peeked around the elevator door to see which room he entered and then followed him.

I decided that the best approach had to be a direct one. I knocked on the hotel door; it opened and before I knew it, I was head over teacups looking up at Man-Mountain. He had sucker punched me, leaving me dizzy as well as the proud owner of what was going to be a beautiful black eye. He pulled me to my feet in one upward motion. I was pinned against the wall and Man-Mountain said, "You have five seconds to tell me who you are and why you're here."

"My friends and I are trying to figure out who murdered Loren Luft's sisters. I am Bill Bennett, the retired sheriff of this county. We're just trying to help Loren and the police."

He seemed to calm down, but his demeanor didn't change much. I had the impression he could take me apart anytime without warning.

"Sit down over there. I'll get some ice."

The large man returned with a bag of ice, which I quickly placed over my eye. It relieved the pain, but didn't begin to relieve my injured pride.

"Who are you?" I asked.

"My name is John Crane. I'm a private investigator," he said.

I said, "Maybe we could work together."

"No. I work alone. Stay out of my way, or I will tear you apart."

"Well, if we can help, you let me know," I uttered

"I have my own style," he said.

"Then we'll work the cases separately. We're not giving up, but we will be sure not to bother you." I said. Under no circumstances did I want a partner for the shiner I was already sporting. I stood up, leaving with the bag of ice firmly in place, closed the hotel room door behind me, exhaling a sigh of relief. Clearly the direct approach hadn't worked.

As I walked past the desk clerk, he gave me a quizzical look. "I forgot to duck," I said, walking out the door.

Back at the Dead River, Dorothy Harris had gone down to play with her granddaughter in the water when she noticed something half-submerged in the weeds. It was a kayak. Assuming that someone had forgotten to tie it up on the beach, she called her neighbor, Sandy Sundell, thinking that Sandy might know something because her husband, Dan, was the Campers' Club president.

'Hello, Sandy, this is Dorothy from next door. How is everything?"

"Good! How are things with you and Stan?

"Good enough! Say… did you lose a kayak? One washed up into the weeds on our shore, and we think it might be yours. "

"No, but I can tell you that the police are looking for one. It might be the one involved in the murder. Call 911 and let them know you found it, " Sandy Sundell said.

"Thanks! I'll do that," Delores said. She dialed 911.

"This is 911. What is your emergency?" the dispatcher asked.

"It's not really an emergency, but I believe the police are looking for a kayak on the Dead River. My granddaughter and I just found one. Maybe one of your deputies should come and look at it?" Dorothy asked.

"We will send a deputy immediately," the dispatcher replied. "What is your location?" Dorothy filled in the details.

Deputy Roads arrived shortly to retrieve the kayak and called it into the station. Upon hearing this Sheriff Remington then made a round of calls to bring the team up to speed.

When the phone rang, I was walking across the Holiday Inn parking lot. "Hello, Bill, this is John. They've found the kayak on the Dead River."

I said "Finally some good news. Pick me up at *Vito's Pizzeria* in a few minutes."

As we headed toward the Dead River, John took a better look

at me and immediately did a double take, then began making comments about spending time with "the Cyclops." What are friends for?

By the time we arrived at Stan and Dorothy Harris' beautiful log cabin on one of the fingers that flows into the Dead River, their beach had become very crowded. We all gathered at the edge of the river to watch Andy Roads pull the kayak out of the mud. "No signs of ownership, or identification," Sheriff Remington said. He and Deputy Roads would deliver it to their forensics department; maybe they could lift some prints. Finding the paddle would have been more helpful. Sometimes, we just couldn't catch a break.

Chapter Nine

Thursday

It was time for a rendezvous. Sally Hofsteder wanted to meet with her lover, Carl Swanson. It was risky, but Sally just had to see him and Carl Swanson had only reluctantly agreed. They picked *Reflections,* a bar that had just opened in Victorious; the new owner, a retired carpenter who had tried retirement, but found that carving duck decoys wasn't all it was cracked up to be, kept it purposely dark inside, designed, I suppose, to enhance the romantic atmosphere. The new owner had a loyal clientele who dropped by to have a few drinks and not be bothered. Sally and Carl believed they could meet and talk without interference.

"You know we shouldn't be meeting like this," Carl stated.

"We have to talk, Carl."

"What we're doing is wrong and it can only lead to trouble."

"But we have to have a plan because I can't go on like this. Milt is going to start suspecting something, I'm a lousy liar, and I can't hold out much longer. "

"All right, we can tell him tomorrow. I'm supposed to meet with him at my office to discuss updates on the variance problem. Come with him and we'll tell him then. It'll be better to do it in my office. He might not make such a scene."

"Okay, I can wait until tomorrow," Sally said.

Carl and Sally gave each other a longing look, but dared not embrace in case someone was watching, then departed separately.

It was time for their weekly ride and the local mountain bikers set off to ride the ORV trails. The weather was changing and there was a chill in the air, but that didn't deter the hearty band of brothers in sweat and mud. They had just completed a major bike marathon last week and, fresh from their success, were eager to hit the trails again. Mile after mile, they pedaled through washed out roads, rugged terrain, and deep puddles, finally reaching the easy power line trail and coasting downhill toward the Dead River.

While enjoying the serene surroundings, one of the elder statesmen of the group, Max Kanton, noticed something floating along the shore. After everyone had weighed in on what it could be, Brad Land, the unofficial leader of the brave comrades, decided that there was only one way to find out. He believed if you didn't come back bloody or wet, it wasn't a good bike ride. He jumped off his bike and waded into the river.

The object was floating in about three feet of water and, with some effort; he pulled out a paddle covered in weeds and mud. They examined it, assuming that, like so many other things that get pulled off the beach by the waves and then caught in the current, it had probably just floated away from some Dead River cottage. They set it against a tree, and Brad said that he'd call around in the morning. After finishing their ride, the brave companions even had time for some cold beers before returning home for the evening.

Back in Needleton, the smell of stale beer followed Denny March out of *Rocky's Bar*. Before he could take a single step, he was in a choke hold that paralyzed him from the neck down. He was gasping for breath when he heard a menacing voice whisper in his ear.

"Move and you're dead. Blink once if you understand," whispered Man-Mountain.

Marsh slowly blinked once, then felt the release of pressure on his neck and dropped to his knees. Furious, thinking that he was the one who did such things to other people; nobody did that to him, Marsh tried to turn around and throw a haymaker. He was quickly punched in the throat and kicked in the right kneecap. The two successive blows put him down; looking up to see a Man-Mountain standing over him, looking him squarely in the eyes, he knew that, for the first time, he was totally out-matched.

"You better start talking, or I'm going to hurt you bad, and I'll enjoy every minute of it," John Crane said.

Denny Marsh said, "Go to hell."

"I've been there already and this time I'll take you with me," said Crane.

Denny Marsh replied, "I'll kill you first."

Marsh made a feeble swing at Crane, but within seconds he was face down in the mud, unconscious. He never had a chance.

Shutting the television off, Loren Luft made a mad dash for the phone. He could hear it ringing somewhere.... under the pillows on the couch, or between the cushions, or even behind it? He found it on the sixth ring.

"Hello?" he said.

"You got the one hundred thousand for me?" asked Man-Mountain?"

Loren asked, "Did you find out who killed my sisters?"

"Good as done," replied John Crane.

Loren Luft asked, "What do you mean? Do you, or don't you, know who killed my sisters?"

"It's just a matter of hours. I've got Marsh and I am *persuading* him to sing a song. He's kind of shy, but I'm using some tactics I learned at Gitmo. I'll let you know when he breaks," replied Man-Mountain to Luft, then the line went dead.

Chapter Ten

Friday

Returning to Mesabi County after his enforced "vacation" from the car dealership, Scott Randall was actually feeling pretty good about himself. He'd been gone for a week to clear his mind, to Tennessee where his sister, Sara, lived with her husband and five children. She was an absolute Bible thumper. There were no gray areas with her. Either you believed in God, or you were going to Hell.

The congregation prayed daily on their knees. Preacher Nelson gave a fire and brimstone sermon every night lasting for hours. Scott Randall didn't care. He needed to be one with God. Scott could remember when he used to make fun of his sister and her religion. Now he realized it was probably the only thing that might save him. Sara quoted the scriptures all day until even he was almost sick of it. He realized God was the only way to salvation. He admitted his most grievous faults in front of the whole congregation.

After each admitted fault, the congregation would shout a mighty "*Hallelujah.*" After what seemed forever, he finally broke down and cried. Sara, Preacher Nelson and the congregation gathered around him, hugging him as he had never been hugged before. He felt cleansed of all his impure thoughts, especially toward Ronnie.

After a heavy week of soul-searching and purifying, he realized that he would have to continue without Ronnie. He didn't know who killed her, but he would have to go on. That's why, upon his return and dismissal from the car dealership, he had felt betrayed. He had tried to get better. He had accepted that he would never be with her. Why was he being punished for trying to become a born again Christian? He put his faith in Jesus, praying even harder.

What he didn't know was that Ronnie had already been involved with someone else. Who would have guessed that it was Milt Hofsteder? Since the first time she saw him, she had adored him. She really liked good-looking older men who had strong personalities and status in the community; after all, Milt was the CEO of a major company. Just the aura around him was electric. When no one was around, she would wander over along his shoreline ... and her strategy worked. He would come out of the house and, since his wife wasn't home, he began asking her to come in for a drink. Soon, "coming in for a drink" became a whole lot more than friendship between them and she began to look forward to their almost daily trysts. The exhilaration was electric. Each time they parted, she tried to make plans to be with him again. All he ever said was, "He'd have to see. After all, he was married." Milt Hofsteder wasn't capable of making a commitment to anyone. He was taking advantage of the opportunity, although he sure didn't feel that the relationship had any long-term future, and he certainly didn't appreciate her planning "their future together."

Hofsteder was scrutinizing his new house plans when the phone rang; all he heard on the other end was: "I know what you did." The line went dead. Who could possibly know he had been having sex with Ronnie McCann? He had actually hoped his wife would be blamed for Ronnie's murder after the police found that golf club key chain at the scene of the crime. He had known for a long time that she was having an affair with Carl Swanson. He wondered why they hadn't found the murder weapon.

Sheriff Remington called me the next day at home. He said, "I just got a call from one of my deputies; the missing kayak paddle has been located. Some mountain bikers found it last night, but they couldn't bring it back on their bikes. I sent Deputy Roads to retrieve it." The sorry looking deputy arrived at the sheriff's office with more mud on him than on the paddle. He was just about the unluckiest man on the planet. We knew it would take days to process, but that was the least of our worries.

Tom McCann examined the paper in his hand one more time. It was a letter that Ronnie had enclosed with the signed divorce papers the week before she was killed. It read:

> *Tom,*
> *You broke my heart when you left. I have had time to think and I no longer oppose the divorce. I've moved on. Actually, I found someone else – Milt Hofsteder. I hope you will be happy for me just like I am happy for you. As you'll see, I signed divorce papers.*
> *Ronnie*

Fortunately, he had kept the precious letter in his pocket, so John and Tyler Baldwin hadn't found it when they searched his hotel room. How stupid did they think he was? Didn't they realize how clumsy they were hiding in the shower stall? He'd had to pretend he was asleep just, so they could slip out. He was a lot smarter than any of them, and he was going to prove it.

It was Saturday morning and only a skeleton crew was working at the Preston and Swanson law office. The Hofsteders kept their appointment with Carl Swanson; Milt guessed that Carl had some news relating to the variance, although the variance problem was the last thing on Carl's mind. He had to convince Milt Hofsteder to give Sally a divorce. Surely, Milt would see they were in love. How could he stand in their way? Carl told his paralegal, Sandy Sundell, to be ready to come into his office if she felt the meeting was getting out of hand. She had done this many times. She smiled, saying she would. Swanson was just going to tell Hofsteder the truth, but he wanted to be ready for the worst.

Sally and Milt entered Carl Swanson's office and sat down. After the usual small talk about river levels and changes in the weather, Carl said:

"Milt, I asked you here along with Sally to tell you that Sally and I are in love. We want to get married. I know this is catching you off guard, but we just wanted to tell you. Can we talk about it?"

The expected explosion didn't come. Milt paused for a moment; deep down, he really wanted to kill them both right there, but he knew he couldn't, not now anyway. That could wait … and he knew how to wait. After several moments, Milt said calmly.

"Sorry, I won't give my wife a divorce,"

Sally started to cry, looking at Carl for help.

Carl said, "I'm sorry Milt, but we are in love and we're going to get married after the divorce. I was hoping we could be civilized about this."

Hofsteder howled, "I will never grant her a divorce. Over my dead body will I ever let her go! I have too much invested in this marriage to let her leave for a simple romantic fling." The truth was that he didn't love Sally – she had only been a trophy wife, but it was a matter of pride. He was not going to be embarrassed by this small town lawyer. As his voice became louder and angrier, Sandy Sundell heard her cue. She had done this many times.

"Coffee anyone?" she asked as she entered the room.

"No thanks. I only socialize with my friends," Milt screamed. He rose, glared at Swanson, gave his wife a threatening look, and stormed out of the office.

Sally burst into tears and wept uncontrollably. Carl came around from behind his desk, knelt down, and put his arm around her shoulder. She laid her head on his shoulder, continuing to sob. Sandy Sundell closed the door behind her. She had seen the scenario play out many times in Swanson's office, only this time she didn't know the whole story.

"Milt will have to give you a divorce. Be patient. We have the rest of our lives to be together," Carl whispered.

"The longer we wait, the harder it will be. Once he gets his dream house built, he will never let me go," Sally said.

"I know you want to be with me as much as I with you," Carl

said with a woeful stare back at her. They embraced, holding each other tight.

By the time `Milt returned home, he was furious. Previously, he had only worried about Ronnie and Nancy's deaths. Now he planned to kill Carl Swanson and his own wife. It wouldn't be hard, though. Drawing on years of work as a chemist before becoming CEO of Pearl, Inc., it would be an easy thing to do. Sally always grew castor bean plants that shaded the south side of the deck all summer long. It had been no problem drying and then grinding up the poisonous seeds –just one milligram of the ricin can kill an adult. He had thought about poisoning Luft to settle the variance issue. Now, he'd bring the poison to the Campers Club Halloween party and drop it into Carl Swanson's drink when he had a chance.

Chapter Eleven

Saturday night

It was late October and the traditional Campers Club Halloween party was being held, as usual, at the St. James' Activity Hall. The gathering offered a welcome chance for everyone to get together before the snowbirds left for the winter. The theme was "dress as your favorite fantasy character." I went as Batman and my lovely wife Barb as Cat Woman. I have to say she was *purrrrfect* for the role. Terri and Dennis Westland were dressed as Raggedy Ann and Andy. Glenn and Cindy Dire came as Mickey and Minnie Mouse. Dan and Shannon Beck came as Captain Jack Sparrow and Angelina, his counterpart, in the movie trilogy *Pirates of the Caribbean*. The Hofsteders were dressed as Hans Solo and a sad looking Princess Leia. Carl Swanson dressed as a Jedi Warrior. For some reason, he steered clear of the Hofsteders. Stan and Dorothy Harris came as Robin Hood and Maid Marian. Kenny and Megan Bievins dressed as Superman and Wonder Woman. The Peanuts characters were all there – Lucy was an old girlfriend I had dated back in high school. She still looked as crabby as her character was. Charlie Brown seemed to be enjoying himself. Six old fashioneds will do that. The Sesame Street characters were also well represented. Big Bird was dancing up a storm with Cookie Monster. I couldn't imagine wearing those costumes all evening. I did notice that Jack Sparrow was going down with the ship. His wife, Angelina, just rolled her eyes as she lifted his car keys from his front pocket and deposited them into her purse

It amazed me that people could block out the recent tragedies. It was freaky to think that the murderer might actually be among us. As people refilled their drinks, the conversation naturally turned to the tragic murders of the two women. Everyone had his or her own suspicions. I decided to keep quiet and listen. You never know who might be able to shed light on the murders.

"I wonder if it could be someone from out of the area. I hate to think it was one of our members," Raggedy Ann said.

"I agree with Raggedy Ann. It has to be a drifter who saw an opportunity and attacked Ronnie," Minnie Mouse said, looking around for affirmation.

"If it was a drifter, why did he come back two days later and kill her sister? It just doesn't make sense," Raggedy Ann said.

"I hate to say it, but I think the murderer is in this room," Maid Marion said, looking at Robin Hood for support.

"I think the sheriff should be doing a better job. He must know who did it. Why doesn't he arrest the murderer? We pay a lot of taxes out here," Wonder Woman said emphatically.

"They can't arrest someone on suspicion alone. They need proof," Hans Solo said, spouting his legal expertise. He looked at me and I nodded.

"They found the kayak on our shore the other day. It has to be one of us," Robin Hood said, surveying the group.

Superman said, "I wonder if it was the husband, Tom McCann. After all, he's back in the area and he has a hell of a motive. He ran out on her once and then she didn't want him back."

Big Bird and Cookie Monster staggered over to our table, falling onto a bench and gasping for air.

Captain Jack Sparrow just sagged onto Angelina's shoulder; it would be a challenge to keep him afloat.

Wonder Woman said, "I read a lot of detective stories, and it's always the person you least suspect."

As the conversation continued, Milt Hofsteder had made his way to the bar, savoring his gin and tonic. His wife, Sally, sat in the corner, looking downcast and on the verge of tears. Milt was waiting for his chance – Carl Swanson would have to come to the bar at some point and order another drink. When Swanson strolled up to the bar, Hofsteder moved in. He removed his Hans Solo mask, saying: "I'm sure we can talk this out."

Swanson replied curtly, "Maybe, but what I said earlier today still goes between Sally and me." Hofsteder could have strangled him right there. As the bartender handed the drink to Carl Swanson and took his money, Hofsteder knew that it was now or never.

"Why don't you go and talk to Sally?" Hofsteder asked. He knew Swanson would look her way, giving him the opening he needed. Swanson fell into the trap. As he gazed longingly at Sally, Hofsteder removed the vial from his costume and dumped the powder into Swanson's drink, chortling to himself that it would be Swanson's last gaze at anyone. As Swanson was bringing the glass to his lips, Jack Sparrow suddenly stood up and staggered toward the bar, knocking the drink harmlessly to the floor. Everyone laughed except Hans Solo, who turned, and for the second time that day, stormed out of a room in a huff, dragging a sobbing Princess Leia with him.

Gary Payne observed it all from the end of the bar, toasting me with a glass of club soda. I smiled, nodding back in acknowledgement. Gary Payne was heading in the right direction and I was happy for him.

Chapter Twelve

Back at the cottage, Loren began sorting through his sisters' clothes, trying to decide what should be donated to St. Vinnies and what should be kept for her daughters. Reaching into the far back corner, something fell onto the floor. To his amazement, it was a golf club and it looked like it was covered in blood. Taped to the club was a blood smeared envelope, which included a used condom and a note, addressed to Scott Randall, in Nancy's handwriting.

My dearest Scott,
I know you won't understand. I have loved you since I first met you. I could hardly keep my feelings to myself. When you were near Ronnie, laughing and enjoying yourself, you tried to be subtle. I wish it could have been you and me. I loved my husband, but I came to adore you, also. You are very sweet. I loved the way you doted on Ronnie. Even though she didn't reciprocate, I was envious. I didn't tell anyone about my feelings for fear it might ruin your relationship with Ronnie. The morning I found my sister dead in her room, I found the bloody golf club and the used condom near her body. I knew it had to be yours, but I didn't want you to get in trouble, so I hid them here. I know you could never hurt Ronnie. You loved her too much. I didn't want you to be accused of the crime. The evidence is safe with me.
Love, Nancy

As Loren folded up the letter, he just could not imagine who could have wanted to hurt either sister. They never harmed anyone and were kind, generous women. It was high time that he took a more active role in finding their killer.

Saturday night
In a garage, John Crane had tied Denny Marsh's hands together
and suspended him from a rope attached to the ceiling.
"Either talk now, or I start the waterboarding. Take your pick,"
John Crane threatened. He started filling a pail with water.
Denny Marsh gasped. "All right, I'll tell you what you want
to know. I can't take it anymore."
John Crane barked, "Who killed the two women?"
"Get me down, and I'll tell you everything."
"No, it doesn't work that way. You tell me everything now, or
you can hang up there until your hands fall off. I could care less
what happens to you."
"I don't know who killed them. I swear it. I was just supposed
to scare Loren Luft into signing the variance. I suppose it had to
be Milt Hofsteder. How did you know I was involved, anyway?"
Man-Mountain said, "I have connections in the FBI. They
checked the Hofsteders' phone calls. They owed me a favor,"
"I told that idiot not to call me," Marsh said. Crane lowered
him to the ground and started to walk away.
"Hey, aren't you going to untie me. I told you everything I
know?" Marsh screamed.
"Nope. You got yourself into this predicament. Now you can
get yourself out," Crane replied.

Chapter Thirteen

It was Monday night and that meant golf. By early November, with full-on winter right around the corner, it was one of the last chances for the season. The sky was clear except for some fluffy clouds floating gently overhead. Over on the putting green, Gary Payne was surprised to see Loren, Ben and Mark show up. In fact, everyone was surprised Loren was there with his two sisters' murders hanging over his head. They asked Gary if he wanted to join them and he willingly agreed, strapping his golf bag onto Loren's cart. As if apologizing, Loren said: "I know this sounds crazy, but I had to get out of the house. I can't stop thinking about my sisters' murders."

"I agree. There's nothing like golf to get your mind off things for a while." Gary replied.

Ben and Mark teed off. Gary's drive went a good hundred yards further; Loren sent his ball long, but over to the right side. As Loren was putting his driver back into the bag, a firecracker exploded; suddenly Gary Payne slumped over in the cart, the back of his head a bloody mess. Ben realized immediately what had happened, screaming for everyone to get down. He called to Gary, but there was no response. Ben dialed 911.

Peering cautiously into the tree line in the distance, they saw nothing unusual. Nobody moved. Rick Bonnetelli and David Lemon, who were playing ahead of them, rushed back to see if they could help, but there was no hope.

On the other side of the tree line, Denny Marsh saw Luft approaching the first tee. It must have been Loren Luft who was responsible for his humiliation. Realizing that he'd missed Luft, he picked up the spent shell, got to his truck, and casually drove away. Marsh would try again when the opportunity presented itself.

Chapter Fourteen

Tuesday evening

Reconvening at *Geno's Pizzeria* and reviewing the terrible events with Rick Bonnetelli; we were all in shock. There were no leads. Even the pizza and beer did little to take our minds off of the horrific things that had happened. Finally, the team got down to business.

"Ben, why don't you keep an eye on Scott Randall? He hasn't moved much in the last few days," I said.

"I will continue to follow Sally Hofsteder." John said. "She met Swanson at *Reflections* Thursday night and checked into the *Holiday Inn* on Friday. Saturday afternoon, she met her husband and together they entered Swanson's law office. He came out steaming a few minutes later, and neither one looked too happy at the Halloween party Saturday night. Last night, she went back to the Holiday Inn and hasn't left there since."

Tyler announced, "I have a few days off, so I can follow Swanson. He seems to be pretty slippery. Two nights ago, he also showed up at *Reflections*. I think there's probably a little hanky-panky behind Hofstadter's back. With Milt's temper, I don't think that's such a good idea."

Mark added, "I will keep an eye on Loren Luft. After his wild threats, he seems to have settled down."

My question was where was Man-Mountain? I only had one good eye left, and I didn't want to see that one closed. "It's as if the Man-Mountain has vanished, I said.

"I think you should make another date with him. That shiner improves your looks," John said.

I said, "I guess that leaves Milt Hofsteder for me." Why do I always get the short straw?

At home, Milt Hofsteder was planning to finish what he had started. If another threatening phone call came, he would be ready. He had a Colt 45 that would do the trick. He just had to make sure the meeting was in a remote area. There were a lot of places along the Dead River that fit that description. With so many hunters in the woods since the opening of small game season on September 15 and with deer season only a few months away, so many would-be hunters were target practicing. Nobody would pay any attention to shots heard in the distance. It would work out; he'd deal with his two-timing wife and lover. They'd pay. They'd all pay.

When the phone rang, the voice on the other end was without emotion.

"You murdered my wife and if you want me to keep quiet, you better come up with a lot of cash. My silence is not going to come cheap. In a letter, Ronnie identified you as the man she loved." Tom McCann threatened.

"How much do you want?" Hofsteder asked, knowing he wasn't going to pay this blackmailer a dime.

The voice said, "It will cost you five hundred thousand dollars in cash. *"*

Hofsteder said, "It will take me several days to get that kind of money. I will have to liquidate my stocks."

McCann said, "I don't care how you get it. Just have the money within forty-eight hours, or the police will have Ronnie's letter."

"I will see what I can do," Hofsteder replied. "Just hold on to that letter… and bring it with you."

Chapter Fifteen

Wednesday evening

Hofsteder would take care of Tom McCann and maybe also take care of the old retired guys and the kid who were nosing around, too. They might actually stumble onto something. Sally couldn't stand any more stress. Hofsteder sure didn't want Bennett and his amateurs going near her; if they pressed her again, she'd fall apart and tell them that he really wasn't with her the night Ronnie McCann was murdered. Then there would be big trouble. The best idea was to eliminate Bennett. If you cut the head off a snake, the body dies. He would shoot the ringleader. That would put some fear into those pseudo-detectives for sure.

No time like the present. He packed his .44 Remington Magnum Carbine, ammunition, and night goggles, and then drove out toward the Bennett's cottage. It was up high and would be hard to approach from the riverside. He would be seen pretty easily. There were cottages on either side, but they'd been empty since the end of the boating season. The dense trees between the cottages provided ample cover. He knew he couldn't park on the road since his Camry could easily be seen by a passer-by, so he coasted into the driveway of one of the deserted cottages. Wearing night vision goggles and sneaking through the woods toward the cottage, Hofsteder could see movement inside: Bennett's wife, Barb, was watching television. Maybe Bill was somewhere else in the house? He would wait. Just then, a car came down the road, turned into the Bennett driveway and parked.

It was Bill Bennett. He entered the cottage, turned on the light in the kitchen, and preceded into the living room, where he sat back in a lazy boy. Hofsteder would have to shoot Barb first; then Bill would stand up to see what happened, and he'd fire off a second shot.

He waited for Barb to lean forward. Just a little more and she'd be dead. Just as he pulled the trigger, she sat back in the chair. The shot missed.

I could see she wasn't hit, but Barb sure was stunned. The loud crack had reverberated through the room like a cannon. We both dove onto the floor, frozen in fear. After several minutes, I got the nerve to look out the window, then grabbed my Glock and the flashlight from the porch windowsill and jumped from the top of the steps to the landing in one leap. I dashed for the woods, hoping that the shooter was still there. I saw a vehicle silhouetted in front of the neighbor's garage, and I fired a shot in that general direction, knowing I had no hope of hitting the would-be assassin.

The headlights came on; the vehicle sped up the driveway and swung around the first curve in the road. There was no point in shooting a second time. It wasn't worth taking a chance.

"What happened?" Barb asked.

"Someone took a shot at us," I said trying to sound confident, but failing.

"Why shoot at us? You're retired. It must be related to Ronnie McCann's and Nancy Mather's murderer. Why would they want to do that?" she asked as she stared at me.

I called 911 and then turned on all the outside lights. Within five minutes a sheriff's cruiser sped down the road with its lights flashing. Deputy Roads leaped out, racing toward the front door.

"How is everyone?" He asked?

"Still shaking, but we're okay. Whoever did it parked in the neighbor's driveway. I fired once, but they got away."

I showed him the bullet hole in the living room window. Sherriff Remington also appeared with his cruiser lights flashing. We retraced my steps through the woods to the neighbors' cottage, and they took a few pictures of the car's tire tracks.

"We should be able to get a make on the vehicle's tires," Remington said to me. "I'll send them into the state police crime lab tomorrow."

"Were you able to see the vehicle?" Sheriff Remington asked. "Not a chance; it was way too dark," I said. I had never been shot at before. It was an eerie feeling and this whole thing had totally destroyed my feeling of security. Other deputies arrived and combed the area for evidence. Sheriff Remington came back inside: "We caught a break," he said, holding up the casing in a cellophane bag. "We'll be back in the morning. Try to get some sleep."

I wish I could say Barb and I had a relaxing night, but I can't. We lay side by side for hours until Barb finally fell asleep. I went out to the lazy boy and stared at the full moon. It should have been a beautiful night on the river, but somehow I could only think about how I was going to kill that person who violated us.

The next morning, car doors slamming awakened us. There must have been an army of forensic experts dressed in blue fatigues. Even though I had conducted dozens of investigations over the years, I should have known better than to try to help. With the experience that a keen retired sheriff possesses, I did the next best thing: I made a pot of coffee for the guys. It was going to be a long morning.

As he left, the sheriff said, "We will do everything we can to catch this person. We have photographs of the tire tracks, the shell we dug out of the wall, and the spent casing. That's a good start."

I had given a similar speech many times myself. I nodded, thanking him as I shook his hand. I gave him a polite wave good-by, as he drove away. "I'll be the one to get this SOB," I said to myself.

Chapter Sixteen

Thursday evening
Two days had passed since our rendezvous at *Geno's Pizzeria*. No progress was being made on the murder investigations. The kayak paddle had either been wiped clean, or was so covered with mud and grime that prints were unobtainable. We were taking turns baby-sitting Hofsteder, thinking he was now our top suspect. It was my turn to take the graveyard shift. I had all the luck.

McCann had called Hofsteder to set up a meeting.

"Let's meet out at the parking lot at the east end of the Dead River," Milt Hofsteder suggested brazenly.

"You've got to be kidding." Tom McCann replied. "I want to meet someplace where I feel safe."

"What about the Victorious Sports Complex. It's pretty deserted this time of year." Hofsteder suggested, thinking he could still get a couple of shots off without any complications.

McCann said, "Nope" disagreeing just because Hofsteder suggested it.

"What about the Victorious playgrounds?" McCann asked.

"Okay, that's pretty deserted. The only people who use it are old timers playing tennis in the summer anyway. With the cold, it's doubtful anyone will be there," Hofsteder responded.

"Be there in one hour, or I'll mail the evidence to the police."

Both hung up simultaneously, thinking how they were each going to kill the other.

I was sitting in my car, doing surveillance and drinking stale coffee. The sun went down early this time of year. It would soon be dark. All of a sudden, Hofsteder's garage door opened. His silver Camry flew out, so fast I barely saw who was at the wheel.

He looked like a madman on a mission. I reversed direction and accelerated. I had to keep up.

I called Baldwin to let him know what was happening. He told me to keep him posted. I knew I could count on him. After all, he and I had been friends for a lifetime and you couldn't put a price on that. I could barely see Hofsteder's vehicle as we sped down the winding county roads. I felt this was coming to a head. Nobody drives that fast unless they're crazy. It was ten miles to town, but we covered it in only a few minutes, even though it had snowed the night before and there were patches of black ice. Hofsteder took some of the sharp curves on two wheels. I slowed down – I was not ready to see the Pearly Gates anytime soon. Why did I always get the short straw?

Hofsteder sped through the residential areas, flying by St. James' Church and the city cemetery, and then blew through the roundabout. I had no choice, but to stop. An eighteen-wheeler was coming up the highway, and I didn't want to become a hood ornament.

Hofsteder disappeared down the dark city street. I followed, guessing his destination, and called John.

"Hello," John answered.

I said, "This is Bill. Can you come to the Victorious Playground? I think it's going down."

John said, "I'll be right there. I'll call the others."

I turned off the car lights and pulled slowly into one of the parking lots. As I prepared to step out of my car, I saw another vehicle approach. Man-Mountain stepped out of his vehicle and aimed a 12-gauge shotgun at Tom McCann and Milt Hofsteder, who were silently faced off on the edge of the parking lot. They put their hands up, stepping apart and backward. Neither wanted any part of Man-Mountain.

Looking at Tom McCann, Crane said in a low, firm voice, "If you don't want to die tonight, get out of here. Now*!*"

Tom McCann left. There was always another day to pick a fight. After all, he still had Ronnie's note –the blackmail money could wait.

As Tom McCann was pulling out of the parking lot, another car pulled up. Loren Luft stepped out of the vehicle. Crane had let him know that he had Milt Hofsteder cornered. Luft approached Hofsteder, a look of hatred in his eyes and a 9 mm pistol in his hand. It was time to act. Racing toward the group, I tackled Luft; we both went sprawling onto the pavement. Crane stood helplessly: with me as a witness, it was obvious that killing Hofsteder wasn't an option anymore.

Then, all hell broke out.

A shot rang out. John Crane, the seemingly indestructible Man-Mountain, jolted back from the impact and grabbed his left shoulder, falling to the ground. He crawled behind his car, returning fire. For several minutes, shots echoed through the playground. Crane maneuvered around to the front of his vehicle, then took aim and fired.

Crane stood and walked toward the body. Loren kept his Colt 45 aimed right at Hofsteder as he and I joined Crane. The shooter was Denny Marsh. He had gotten himself untied and followed Crane, hoping to get revenge on the man who had ruined his reputation as the countywide enforcer for hire.

Almost simultaneously, law enforcement vehicles approached with their lights flashing and the neighbors quickly gathered; front porch lights blazed all around the park.

They were followed by the Baldwin's, Mark, and Ben. That was enough for John Crane, who was bleeding from the shoulder wound. He looked at Loren Luft and said, "I knew it was worth following Tom McCann. Now, I made good on my guarantee, Luft. You owe me the balance. Don't forget." He got into his car, and sped away into the darkness.

Sheriff Remington said, "We can take it from here. Andy, put Hofsteder in custody and read him his rights. Call an ambulance."

Milt Hofsteder put his hands up and was handcuffed, then tucked into the back seat of his cruiser. Hofsteder had a blank look on his face. I had seen it many times.

"Why didn't you call me?" Sheriff Remington asked me.

"I didn't have time. I had Hofsteder under surveillance; I

barely had time to call John."

"Next time, we might not come," Sheriff Remington snarled.

"I know you will. You'd miss me too much," I said.

"Get on home. You're starting to annoy me," Sheriff Remington said.

We shook hands and I just smiled in response

Chapter Seventeen

Milt Hofsteder admitted to both murders. In the spring, he was tried and convicted. Tom McCann made good on his threat – Ronnie's incriminating letter identifying Hofsteder as her lover arrived in Sheriff Remington's in-box just before the trial started. During the trial, Hofsteder admitted that he purposely left the key chain and a used condom to incriminate his wife and also used his wife's golf club to kill Ronnie McCann. He had also set the kayak and paddle adrift in the hopes of misleading the authorities. His plan almost worked.

When the club went missing, he was sure that Nancy Mather was on to him. Who else could have hidden it? In the end, one senseless rape and murder had led to another murder, leaving four young children motherless. Gary Payne, an innocent bystander, was also dead. As for Denny Marsh, maybe he just got what he deserved.

As we left the courthouse, Loren Luft was waiting.

"Justice was done, but it will never replace their mother," Loren said.

I was at a loss for words. Barb's eyes welled up; we both nodded.

Chapter Eighteen

After another long winter, the Superior Peninsula was coming alive. The birds had come north again. The mother goose had a new gander of goslings and it was a beautiful spring morning. John, Tyler, Mark, Ben and I were fishing on my pontoon boat, enjoying the comradery, when Mark hooked something big. Another body – Lord knows we had seen enough death to last us a lifetime – although fish and time had done their job and it was impossible to identify. Ben called 911 and we let the professionals take over.

Back at the cottage, we cooked our catch, and after we had finished, we lay on the loungers, looking up at the sky.

"Do you think it gets any better than this?" Mark asked.

"I don't think so," Ben said.

Two eagles glided overhead. They surveyed the land below, then turned and majestically flew away. "Rest in peace, girls," I said.

The next day, Sheriff Remington appeared once again in our driveway.

"Sheriff! Want some coffee? "I asked.

"No, thanks. I'll take a rain check. That body... it was John Crane. Marsh's shot last fall must have been fatal," Sheriff Remington said. "No idea how he ended up in the river. There was an envelope in a water-proof bag containing a check for $200,000, and a note giving the money to the Luft children."

Maybe some things do work out after all.

Loren Luft adopted Nancy's four children, completely changing his solitary bachelor existence. With ample advice – some wanted and some not, some good and some not so good– he had a crash course in parenting and was the frequent recipient of home-cooked meals. People are good.

Ben won the Gitchigoomie Senior Golf Club Championship the next year. Sally Hofsteder and Carl Swanson were married in Las Vegas. They never returned to the Superior Peninsula. Left without a job when Carl Swanson moved away, Sandy Sundell returned to law school and became a partner in the firm where she had previously served as a paralegal. Scott Randall got his job back at the car dealership, and became a lay minister at the Victorious Free Spirit Church, where on summer Sunday mornings, anyone passing by could hear some serious *"Hallelujahs"* and *"Amens."*

The rest of us returned to our daily round of activities, gathering now and again for beer and pizza, satisfied that we had played key roles in resolving the *Murders on the Dead River.*

Part II

The Deer Trail Murders

Chapter 1

The leaves were coming down; if you listened, you could hear them as they landed, then swirled across the dry ground. Everything looked so different. In the summer, most of the cottages on the Dead River were nestled in the dense foliage. Now that the trees were nearly bare, only the pines offered a touch of green. Since most of the cottages were shuttered until next spring, one felt quite alone.

My wife, Barb, and I were enjoying our retirement years. Every season brought new activities. I was particularly looking forward to November: In Michigan, deer season starts on November 15. During the two ensuing weeks, millions of dollars are pumped into the state's economy under the guise of sportsmanship. Friends and family members – mostly guys, of course – set up camp, often in someone's cottage; delicious meals are served; liquid refreshments are consumed; and stories of deer camps past are told around the hearth, or campfire. Every year, a new tale, or two becomes the stuff of legend. When it came to hunting stories, the truth was always exaggerated.

Truth be told, preparation always started months in advance. Trail cameras are placed at strategic locations along the deer trails; pulling the chip allows the recordings to be easily and regularly reviewed. Old gear must be replaced and maybe a new rifle purchased, even if it isn't really necessary; hunting magazines always sing the praises of a "can't miss" new weapon, and everyone always hopes that they'll be the one to bring the biggest buck back to camp.

Our cottage on the Dead River provided a place for quiet relaxation as well as frequent, large-scale celebrations in the summer. It also offered a great retreat from the elements during hunting season in the fall. I had been hunting with friends Mark Kestila, Ben Myers, and John Baldwin for many years. For the last several years, John's son Tyler Baldwin had joined us. At the end of the summer, our neighbor Dr. LaBatt had sold his cottage, but we hadn't met, or even seen, the new owners, what a surprise, then, when we heard shooting next door. Racing outside, to our amazement we saw that one of the new owners had set up beer bottles and was target practicing from his deck. Needless to say, this had to be discouraged – target practice is not permitted within four hundred and fifty feet of an inhabited residence. It appears that he was trying to improve his aim by consuming ample quantities of beer.

We called out to him; when he acknowledged us, we walked over to explain the situation and introduce ourselves. "Sorry," he responded. "I'm trying to get ready for tomorrow. I just can't wait."

An older man came out of the cottage and joined the conversation. "Hello, I'm Wendel Wylie and this is my son Beau. Sorry for my son's behavior. I just bought the cottage from Dr. LaBatt and this is our first time in the Superior Peninsula. We're pretty excited to be able to hunt along the Dead River. They say that some big deer are taken out here."

"That's right," Mark Kestila answered. "Some have even scored in *Boone and Crocket.* You might have first-timers' luck and, be rewarded with the big one."

We invited them over for a cold beverage. The conversation was animated and they were glad to stay on for a taste of Mark's famous deer camp stew. The season was off to a good start.

It was still pitch black the next morning when Tyler served up breakfast. Traditions differ, but in our group, the youngest is always the designated camp cook. We finished off skillet-fried eggs with toast and, just before sunrise, we headed our separate ways, each of us heading out to our preferred good-luck location. After hunting together for years, we all knew exactly the location of each member of our group. If there was a shot, we would know who had fired it and in which direction we should head to help out. With their military training, some of the guys swore that they could even tell the caliber of the rifle.

"I should have mine in a few minutes," Mark said.

"You couldn't hit the broadside of a barn, you old coot," Ben retorted.

"Just wait for my shot. Give me a few minutes, then you can help drag my prize-winner back to camp," Mark said.

"The only thing you'll be dragging back to camp is your sorry ass," John said.

I walked slowly down the trail toward my favorite area of our hunting parcel, being sure not to step on branches and crackle the leaves. I needed to get to my blind without being detected: if I wasn't careful getting there, I would hear a deer snort, followed by the pounding of a hoof to warn the other deer of danger; in a flash, they'd all be gone.

I always sit on the side of a hill facing the wind, about half way up under cover of some prearranged dead branches in as comfortable a spot as possible; I was going to be there for a good many hours. If it was foggy, rainy or snowing, my chances of seeing deer were pretty good. The enemy was wind – deer hated it. It took away one of their natural defenses and in the wind they became very skittish. We old deer hunters know how to use the elements to our advantage.

As the sun rose, I enjoyed the quiet – I could hear everything and was sure that the deer could hear and smell everything, too. They'd be on the move soon, moseying along toward a sunny glade on the side of the hills where they'd spend the afternoon in their "day beds." Hours passed and I was getting ready to call it quits, when I heard something over the rise. I raised my .308, slowly pulling back the hammer. It was a beautiful ten point buck – the same one I'd been watching on my trail cams since early fall. I raised my rifle, slowly taking aim, then squeezing the trigger. The buck leaped then dropped. It was a clean shot.

John and Tyler gave me a hand dressing the deer and dragging it back to camp. Always a fierce competitor, John kept saying it wasn't much of a deer. I knew better. We raised it on the buck pole, with a shot of whiskey all around to celebrate. It didn't get any better than this; although John kept mumbling "It really wasn't much of a deer."

Gazing down at the river, whiskey in hand, Tyler rose and pointed at something that was stuck on a sandbar. Perhaps it was a log or clump of floating weeds? Maybe even a dead deer? A wounded animal would try to escape even if it meant crossing open water. We rowed out to investigate, and, as we got closer, it became apparent that it was a body. To our horror, it was a woman. We brought it to shore and immediately called 911.

"I think I recognize her. Isn't she the local news reporter from Channel Seven," Ben said.

Soon, Deputy Roads' cruiser could be seen approaching with the flashers on and shortly afterward, other police vehicles arrived. The former medical examiner, Doc Stevens, had retired since our previous investigation, and the new M.E. was not at all what we envisioned. Her name was Carolyn Raft and she was downright gorgeous. She had blond hair that cascaded down her back and her blue eyes accented her whole face. Tyler certainly seemed interested! As the rest of us headed back to the cottage, Tyler mentioned that he had something more to say to the medical examiner. Perhaps he wasn't interested only in the case.

The two-week hunting season came to an end all too soon. John did get a buck that had never showed up on any of my trail cams. Naturally, he had to gloat that the rack was much larger than the one that I'd bagged. Two nice bucks in the same season would provide plenty to brag about and compare for years to come. Such is deer camp.

Upon our return to civilization, we were intrigued by the murder. I perused the newspapers over the next two weeks, catching up on world and local events. Of course, the main local story was the young female's murder. The victim had been shot; the police did not release any information. Ben was correct in his early prediction. The victim was the news reporter from Channel Seven, Cindy Mason. She had been the anchor person for the local news for several years and was very good. Usually, when reporters are smooth and professional they leave our small-town market and move on to larger television stations. Unfortunately, she would never get that chance. *The Mining Ledger* and Channel Seven were putting pressure on the police to solve the murder.

Chapter Two

In addition to being my hunting buddies, Mark, Ben, John and Tyler are also my compatriots in detection. Each of us is currently involved in, or retired from, some position in law enforcement. Mark Kestila and Ben Myers arrived at *Geno's* together. John and Tyler Baldwin followed. The proprietor, Rick Bonnetelli, was behind the bar: he knew we were good for a few pizzas and several cold pitchers of beer. We took a booth in the back. Sometimes, we overstayed our welcome.

"So what do we know about Cindy Mason?" I asked.

Tyler Baldwin said, "I have seen her more than a few times in *Rocky's Bar* in Needleton when I make my rounds at night. I could ask the owner, Tom Timmerman, more about her."

"Mark and I could check with the television personnel," Ben chimed in.

"John and I could check with the medical examiner. Maybe, if we use our natural charm we could glean some information from her," I said.

"If it's okay with you, I'd like to take my dad's place on that visit," Tyler said. Tyler really seemed to approve of the new M.E

I said, "Sure, I will pick you up in the morning."

We departed, agreeing to meet the following Monday night to compare notes.

The next morning, Tyler and I entered the Mesabi County Sheriff Department and we headed for the medical examiner's office. I took the lead and introduced Tyler and myself in case she had forgotten our names.

"Hello, my name is Bill Bennett. We met at my cottage on the Dead River a few weeks ago," I added hoping that she'd remember us. "I retired from my post as sheriff two years ago.

You remember Tyler Baldwin, right? He's a Needleton police sergeant." I hoped my former connection to the law enforcement might open some doors involving the crime. She smiled, but didn't seem impressed.

Carolyn said, "Don't even ask. I'm sorry, but you know that I can't release any information that isn't cleared through Sheriff Remington. Now, if you will excuse me, I have to get back to work."

As Tyler turned to leave, he saw a tray with a few dissecting tools and some papers on the edge of the counter. He nodded toward them; I discreetly moved my head up and down, and with a crash, the instruments hit the floor.

Scolding Tyler like a child, they scrambled to pick up the utensils and scattered paperwork. It was almost comical watching them crawl around on the floor. Tyler actually kept trying to move things farther away rather than trying to retrieve them. His antics gave me vital time to glance at some of the medical examiner's reports on Carolyn's desk. Knowing just where to look on the form, I saw that the shot came from a single .22 caliber pistol and passed through the aorta, making death instantaneous. The bullet had been sent upstairs to forensics. There were also cuts and bruises on the hands and arms which could have been defensive abrasions. Tyler was attempting to apologize. As we stepped cautiously toward the exit door, thanking her for her time, Tyler asked, "And is there a Mr. Raft?"

"I'm divorced," she replied. "I left Lower Michigan to get a new start on life."

Tyler asked, "Could I see you sometime?"

"I'm pretty busy. If we have a drink, would you spill it on me?" she asked in reply.

Tyler said, "Not a chance. I'll call you."

"We'll see," Carolyn said coyly.

That night, Tyler was making his rounds with a younger officer, Steve Dalrymple. Entering *Rocky's*, Officer Dalrymple headed immediately to check out the bathrooms. When looking for illegal activities in the bar, the bathrooms are always a good place to start. Meanwhile, Tyler slowly moved to the end of the bar, motioning to Tom Timmerman. Timmerman glanced around the bar; hesitating as he left the conversation he was having with a lady.

"Did you know Cindy Mason?" asked Tyler, looking at Timmerman for a reply.

Timmerman said, "She was in here off and on."

"That's not what I asked you," Tyler replied staring Timmerman in the eyes.

Timmerman became more defiant. "I don't have to answer that because it's not your jurisdiction. The sheriff is handling the investigation. Now leave me alone."

Tyler said, "Okay. If that's the way you want to go, we can start checking ID's, and I think I'll start with that young couple over in the corner."

Timmerman said, "Okay. Okay. Back off. Yes, I knew her. Cindy Mason was in here almost every night."

"Did she hang out with anyone special?" Tyler asked.

Timmerman said, "Not really. She liked to play the field. Now will you get out of here?"

Officer Dalrymple returned from the bathrooms. "Clean for now," he grunted. The officers left and Timmerman breathed a sigh of relief.

Throughout the whole conversation, two men had purposely kept their backs turned, although they had been close enough to Tyler and Timmerman to hear every word. After the officers had departed, the two men, Spike Jankowski and Beau Wylie, approached Timmerman. Jankowski had belonged to a white supremacist ring. He was huge, with gang tats on both arms. Timmerman actually knew Wylie pretty well. His father, Wendel, had been a heavy drug dealer north of Detroit. Rumor was he was second in command of the drug cartel in Lower Michigan. Both Wylies and Spike Jankowski had come to the Superior Peninsula when they began to feel that the FBI were starting to close in on them downstate. A snitch had agreed to testify against the Wylies, but before he could testify, he was found dead with his throat slit.

Beau Wylie said, "Listen up, old man. You did good, real good, just keep your mouth shut about everything if you want to live." Both Beau Wylie and Spike Jankowski gave an evil stare toward Timmerman as they left. Once they were gone, Timmerman picked up his phone and made a call.

The next afternoon, Mark Kestila and Ben Meyers paid a visit to Channel Seven to see what they could find out about Cindy Mason. The station was located just east of Needleton. Upon entering, they had to wait as the receptionist was on the telephone. They read the name *Debbie Kinsely* on her name plate. Some time passed, giving them a chance to examine the walls decorated with the local television personalities' pictures. Cindy Mason's photograph had black bunting draped over it. After the receptionist hung up she asked, "What can I do for you?"

Ben asked, "We would like to talk to the station manager regarding Ms. Mason."

"The sheriff's deputies were already here several days ago. I believe that he answered all their questions," stated the receptionist professionally.

"Yes. We know. We'd just like to speak with the station manager, or with anyone else who is available," Mark stated again.

"I doubt if they're available, but I will see," she replied.

She pressed the intercom button. "Yes, Mr. Cotter? This is Debbie; there are two gentlemen here who would like to speak with you regarding Cindy's death. No, they're not with the police," Debbie said, "Okay, I'll send them in." She pressed the button under her desk, opening the door. "Go on down the hall' it's the last door on the left," she said.

Mark and Ben thanked her. Upon entering the station manager's office, they were taken aback at how small it was. There was barely enough room for the manager's desk and a few chairs. It wasn't at all the glamorous office suite that they had expected.

"Hello, Mr. Cotter. I'm Mark Kestila and this is Ben Myers."
Pete Cotter said, "Have a chair. I'm the station manager here
at WQPF. While I'm happy to see you, I really don't think I
should say anything about Cindy Mason since you're not with
the police." He knew he had to weigh every word. He didn't
know these two would-be detectives, and he certainly wasn't
going to divulge anything that could hurt the station.

"We're just trying to help the police find Ms. Mason's
murderer," Ben said, as if that would make it okay for Cotter to
release information.

"I'm sorry, but I gave the sheriff's detectives all the information
I had. I'm only talking to you as a courtesy," Cotter said.

"Well…," Mark stalled, "Did she socialize with anyone here?"

"I don't know for sure. You might ask Debbie, our receptionist.
They went to school together. I think they went to the bars a few
times," Cotter said.

"Did she have any male friends at the station?" Ben asked
hoping to hear more.

"I don't think so. I believe our sports announcer, Jack Cannon,
talked to her during station breaks, but I don't think she saw him
outside the station," Cotter said. He was hoping to wrap things
up before it turned into a full-fledged inquisition. When it was
clear that he was unable – or perhaps unwilling—to say more,
Mark and Ben thanked him for his time and left. As they walked
down the hall, Mark looked at Ben and said, "He definitely
knows more than he's letting on."

"I agree," Ben said, "Let's see what the receptionist has to
say."

On their way out, they approached Debbie at her desk in the
lobby and said, "Mr. Cotter said you knew Ms. Mason well.
We really would appreciate your help. Can we ask just a few
questions?"

"I don't want to get in trouble, and I don't want to lose my
job," Debbie said.

"If you were a friend of Ms. Mason's, you owe it to her to help
us find her killer" Ben pointed out gently.

"I don't know," Kinsely said.

Ben asked, "Can you live with yourself if her killer goes unpunished?"

"Okay. Fine. I can meet you later tonight at *Rocky's*. These walls have ears. I'll be there about ten o'clock. You gotta believe that I'll deny everything if you repeat anything I say," Debbie said looking at the office entrance door.

Back at the Wylie cottage, Beau Wylie and Spike Jankowski parked their Harleys. Neither one wanted to be the first to go through the door and face Wendel Wylie. He was glaring at them with an angry look in his eyes.

"Timmerman just called me. He told me the Needleton police are still asking around about Mason's death," Wylie barked.

"Don't worry. We were there when the cop cornered him and then we talked to Timmerman. He won't be saying anything to the cops," Beau said.

"He better not, because we got a good thing going here. Out here, with the whole river almost deserted except for old Bill and Barb next door, we can make meth in the back bedroom and nobody'll be the wiser. Now that deer season is over, it's all fine and good. Now, get yourselves back into Victorious, and pick up these ingredients. We're running low, and I want to make a new batch tomorrow." Wylie snarled.

"And take that junk out back, and get rid of it way back in the woods. And take this bag of garbage to some dumpster," ordered Wendel Wylie. They did as they were told. Leaving the cottage, Spike said, "I hate this job."

"Yeah." Beau replied, "And I don't know why should we take this stuff and dump it miles away? It's going to snow soon, so it will be covered up anyway." Driving to the end of the driveway, they turned onto Camp Road. Noticing a logging road that veered off to the left, Beau Wylie said, "Let's just dump it in that clearing back in there."

Jankowski nodded, "Good idea. Nobody will see it until spring and by then we'll probably be gone." They backed up into the clearing, opened the tailgate and shoved the debris into a heap in the woods. They didn't know there would be serious consequences for their actions.

Chapter Three

That evening Debbie Kinsely entered *Rocky's Bar* and took a seat in the back corner. She had gotten there early so she could find an inconspicuous place to meet the pseudo-detectives. There were plenty of places. It was ladies' pool night and the women were gathered around the tables, watching every shot. She didn't have long to wait. Mark Kestila and Ben Myers entered, sized up the room, and then made their way to the back corner booth. The ladies barely gave the two old timers a glance before getting quickly back to their game. It was like they were invisible. Maybe they were.

Joining Debbie, there was a moment of silence, as all three considered what to say.

"Did you know Cindy Mason well?" Ben asked

"We sort of knew each other. I mean, we hung out together a little," she replied.

Mark and Ben could see that they would have to coax the information out of her.

Ben asked, "How well did you know her?"

Debbie Kinsely said, "We'd meet here and sometimes we'd just have a few drinks. With Cindy, we usually didn't have to wait long before guys would start buying us drinks. I got to drink free all night, or until she left with someone."

"Did she leave with different guys or usually the same guy?"

"She used to date Steve Lemke; he's about our age – in his early thirties – and good looking. You know that he had been a star on Victorious' football team years ago except that nobody cared anymore about all of that except him. Whenever, he was in *Rocky's Bar*, he'd bring up his high school sport record. People just shrugged their shoulders and ignored him. More recently, he was the envy of everyone here at *Rocky's* for hooking up with the local celebrity. However, Cindy Mason grew tired of him. Lately it's been all Beau Wylie," Debbie whispered, making sure nobody heard her.

Both Mark and Ben looked at each other with a knowing look.

"How did Lemke take being dumped for Beau Wylie?"

"Not very well. I think that Lemke still had a crush on Cindy Mason even after she broke his heart, but Beau Wylie is a very dangerous young man. I think Lemke was afraid of him."

"Do you think Steve Lemke could hurt Cindy Mason?"

"I don't know. I suppose anything is possible, but he was in love with her until Beau Wylie came along."

"How did Beau Wylie treat her?" Ben's old detective skills were now coming out.

"He was pretty jealous. He didn't like it if she talked to other guys. Sometimes, he would hit her, so hard she had to wear extra make-up when she did her on-air reports," Debbie said. She stared at the pool ladies, making sure none of them were listening.

Ben asked, "Did he ever threaten to kill her?"

"Yes. He said if she ever slept with another guy, it would be the last time." After a pause, she grabbed her purse and got up. "I have to go. I've said too much already." She walked out the back door with her head down.

As Mark and Ben walked out the front door, none of the women even looked in their direction.

The next day, Mark and Ben paid another visit to the television station. Debbie was at her desk in the reception area. Ben asked, "Is it okay if we talk to Cindy Mason's co-workers?"

"I suppose it would be okay," Debbie Kinsely reached under her desk, pressing the button. The door popped open. "Take a right turn and go down the hall. Their dressing rooms are on the left."

"Thanks," Ben said. In the first dressing room, they observed the sports announcer, Jack Cannon, admiring himself in the mirror.

Ben said, "Sorry to bother you, but I'm Ben Myers, and I am a big fan of yours. You do a great job with the sports. This is Mark Kestila. We're trying to help the local police solve Cindy Mason's murder. Do you have a few minutes?"

Jack Cannon looked in the mirror one more time, and then asked, "If you're not police officers, what are you doing here?" Mark said, "We actually are retired law enforcement officers. We're just trying to help."

Jack Cannon said, "Well, I suppose we can give you a few minutes. I have to shoot a promo in a little while."

As they walked toward the studio, Ben asked: "What do you know about Cindy Mason's murder?" Jack Cannon glanced over at Lana Kanton; she had been WQPF's weather girl for years and Jack had been the on-air sports announcer almost as long. Along with Cindy Mason, the three of them did a very professional job but Jack was ready to move on. He had covered every little league, junior high and high school event as well as every team awards program and ribbon cutting for every improvement to the sports facilities and parks for years and years. He was sick of it. All it would take is one big sports story and he could get picked up by a major network. The problem was, major sporting events just didn't happen in the Superior Peninsula.

Jack Cannon said, "Cindy Mason was a true professional. She was a tenacious reporter, and Lana and I have wondered if she'd been close to breaking a big story, but paid for it with her life."

Lana said, "I think she knew who the big drug dealer was in Mesabi County."

Jack added, "But she always kept everything a secret until she was ready to go on-air with it."

"She kept a journal, you know, but after she was murdered it disappeared. I wonder what happened to it." Lana commented.

"The murderer probably took it with him," said Jack Cannon. "We'll probably never find it."

Lana replied, "I told the sheriff's detectives what I know, but I don't want to end up like Cindy. She must have gotten into something over her head. Why else would she end up floating in the Dead River?" Jack Cannon just sadly shook his head.

"Thanks for your time," Mark said.

Meanwhile, Spike and Beau, used a standard operating procedure. After dumping the garbage, they hit the local hardware store for acetone and drain cleaner. The Freon came from an auto parts store and a local junkie was hired to buy the ephedrine, benzene, and ether from the pharmacy in the mall. You just had to sign your name for the pseudoephedrine, so if they only did it occasionally, and didn't go to the same pharmacist too often, the pharmacies didn't catch on. The police checked every month, but fake ID's are easy to come by. If the police got too close, Spike or Beau just made sure the junkies would disappear. Problem solved.

After filming the promo and finishing for the day, Jack Cannon headed over to the new lounge, *Reflections*. The owner, John Canyon, kept the lights low, so that people could have some drinks and enjoy a private conversation without being disturbed. The approach seemed to work.

Jack Cannon approached Debbie Kinsely. "We shouldn't meet like this. I'm a celebrity in this town, and people will wonder what we're doing here when we can talk any time at work," Jack said.

"Well, I'm not going to get in trouble for this. If I go down, you do also," Debbie Kinsely responded. "You were the last person to see Cindy alive. I left after we had done our thing on the beach. I never saw her again."

"Listen, Debbie. I didn't kill her. I left her alive at the river. You've got to believe me. She was going to meet Beau later that night, to pick up more meth. He probably killed her. You know he has a terrible temper. He's a dangerous man," Jack Cannon said.

"Okay, it shouldn't take too long for the police to look in his direction. I already proposed to those two old guys, Kestila and Myers, to consider him a possible suspect. For good measure, I also told them she used to date Steve Lemke. That gives the cops two credible suspects. There ought to be circumstantial evidence to keep them focused on Wylie, or Lemke for a good long while," Debbie said.

Jack Cannon rose, keeping his head down as he left. Debbie ordered another vodka gimlet. Minutes later, she started crying, remembering the good times she and Cindy Mason had together. Cindy had been like a sister to her. She and Cindy would talk for hours about their hopes and dreams. They laughed about their old school days – they first met on the steps as they entered kindergarten. They teased each other about their prom dates and how awful their dresses were. The memories were wonderful. And she really felt bad about having introduced Cindy to Beau Wylie this past summer. She and Cindy had been sitting at the bar when Beau came over and bought them a drink. He could be really charming when he wanted. Before long, Beau and Cindy were together all the time and Steve Lemke was forgotten. She just felt strongly that Beau was involved in the murder. While she wasn't sure who killed her friend, she knew she had to be on guard to protect herself.

Chapter Four

It was Friday morning and another week had passed with nothing concrete to show for it. I thought I might make a second run at Carolyn Raft by myself. I entered the Sheriff's Office as unceremoniously as possible, using the back stairway, so as to avoid meeting any old acquaintances. Looking in the lab, I saw Carolyn was working alone. Well, here goes nothing, I thought to myself.

When entering, I tried to be as chipper as possible. She barely looked up.

"Good morning," I said with a big smile.

Carolyn said curtly, "Busy today with lots of paperwork to do, and I don't have time for amateur detectives. Don't let the door hit you on the way out."

"Come on! Let's be friends. Can't you help an old sheriff?" I asked.

"Good-bye!" Carolyn said emphatically.

Since kindness didn't seem to work, maybe bribery would.

"Did you know Billy Joel was coming to the Mesabi Municipal Theater next week?" I asked.

"Sure, everyone knows that," she replied, "It's been sold out for months. Now get out."

"What if I could get two tickets in the tenth row, center section?"

"Are you kidding me?" Carolyn replied.

Sometimes sacrifices had to be made.

"I have them right here," I said, pulling the tickets out of my wallet.

"What do you want to know?" Carolyn asked.

"How long was the body in the water, and what did the

toxicology report show?" I asked.

Carolyn said, "She was in the water less than twenty-four hours, and she had meth in her system," Carolyn snapped the Billy Joel tickets out of my hand.

I left with the information I needed. I had no clue about how I'd explain the "lost" tickets to my wife Barb.

When leaving the Sheriff's Office, I noticed deputies running to their cars and speeding away with lights flashing. I felt compelled to follow.

I followed the cruisers to the scene of a ghastly crime. Making my way through the crowd in front of *Rocky's* bar, I saw Tyler and his partner, Officer Dalrymple, standing alongside a body in the side alley. The medical examiner pulled up; Dr. Carolyn Raft was all business, but as she passed me, I whispered, "Elton John is coming next month." She cracked a smile, then knelt down and examined the body.

I called John, Mark and Ben to bring them up to speed. John Baldwin arrived first, pushing his way through the crowd. He went right to his son and asked, "Are you okay?" Tyler nodded, and then told him that someone had anonymously phoned in the murder early this morning.

Tyler said, "It looks like Debbie Kinsely. She took one shot through the heart. She was a receptionist for Channel Seven and a good friend of Cindy Mason's. We have to go on the assumption the deaths may be related." It was getting more complicated by the minute.

Worried that Timmerman would certainly have to talk to the police about a body that was found right outside his bar, Beau Wylie and Spike Jankowski decided to pay him another visit. Pulling up to *Rocky's,* they saw a crowd of curiosity seekers in the alley; Timmerman was sitting alone in a booth inside. With the excitement outside, nobody wanted to drink. That would come later.

"What happened in the alley?" Beau asked.

"Looks like someone killed that receptionist from Channel 7," Timmerman said.

"No kidding. Now who would do something like that?" Spike asked sarcastically.

"We're here to reinforce our message in case you were having second thoughts. Don't talk to the cops about anything. You're getting your share of meth to sell; in fact, we should have some more tomorrow. Do you understand?" Beau asked.

"I understand, but if I go down, everyone is going down with me," Timmerman warned.

In response, Jankowski slammed Timmerman's head into the table: "We don't like threats. You talk; you end up like Mason. Understand?" Timmerman nodded.

Chapter Five

The next evening Tom Timmerman drove out to Wylie's cottage. The father-son team along with Jankowski made him very nervous. They were like Dr. Jekyll and Mr. Hyde, friendly and cooperative one minute and pointed a gun at your head the next. He reluctantly knocked on the door.

"Who is it?" asked the voice on the other side.

"It's me, Tom Timmerman. I'm here to pick up the package."

"Just a minute," came the voice on the other side.

The door slowly opened a crack. The man on the inside peeked to make sure Tom Timmerman was alone.

"You can't be too careful," said the voice.

As the door opened a little wider Tom could see Steve Lemke. Apparently Steve couldn't find work anywhere else so he decided to work for Wendel Wylie. And since he had dated Cindy Mason, Steve was also under suspicion for murder.

Lemke said, "Wylie made a large batch. It looks good. Do you want to try some?"

"No, thanks," Timmerman answered.

"Where is Wylie?" Timmerman asked trying to change the subject.

"He's out back getting everything packaged up. The boys are helping him. Have a seat. It won't be long."

Wendel Wylie entered the cottage and smiled at Tom Timmerman. "I heard they had some more trouble in town yesterday. Sure is unusual, two women being killed within a month. This place is getting almost as dangerous as Detroit," Wylie spoke looking at Tom Timmerman with raised eyebrows.

"That's enough with the games. Do you have my stuff, or not?" Timmerman barked.

"Now that's not very neighborly. I was just trying to make polite conversation. What do you think, boys?"

At that instant Beau Wylie and Spike Jankowski entered the room.

"Sit down, Timmerman; we're going to have a little talk. I don't like it when a body ends up next door to my distribution center. It attracts unnecessary attention. Do you understand?" Wylie threatened.

"I had nothing to do with the murder. I can't help it if some bimbo got herself killed outside my bar," Timmerman replied, wishing he had never come through the door.

"The boys have already loaded the meth in your car. That makes two hundred thousand dollars you owe me. You're behind already in your payments. Am I supposed to give you another shipment without any money down? You don't leave without paying. Spike, bring the wire cutters; Beau, check if he has some money on him," Wylie bellowed. Beau searched Timmerman, but found no money. Spike returned with the wire cutters.

"You know I don't have that kind of money," Tom Timmerman replied. "I will wire it to your account tomorrow."

"I think you need a little incentive," Wendel Wylie snorted. He grabbed Timmerman's left hand.

"Wait. Stop. I promise I'll wire it. You can trust me," Timmerman squealed.

The thugs each grabbed an arm and held Timmerman down. Wylie placed the wire cutters over the last joint of his left little finger. Wylie squeezed his fist together compressing the blades. Timmerman let out a scream. Steve Lemke looked away.

"There. I've made my point," Wylie said with a smile. "Give him a towel and get him out of here. Make sure the money is in my account on Monday," Wylie snarled.

Jankowski and Wylie shoved Timmerman out the door. He threw himself into his car, started the engine and drove off, muttering to himself, "I'll get them if it's the last thing I do."

Timmerman pulled into the alley behind his bar. He slammed

the car door and staggered inside. The pain was intense - almost too much to bear. Sweat was pouring down his face. He'd call Connie, his former wife. She was a nurse, and he knew she would come.

"Hello," Connie said.

"Connie, this is Tom. Could you come right away?" Timmerman asked.

"What is it? I'm ready for bed," Connie answered.

"Someone cut the end of one of my fingers off and I'm bleeding," Timmerman whispered.

"How did it happen? Did you call the police? Let me take you to the emergency room," Connie said.

"No, I don't want the police involved, and I can't go to the hospital. Please come now," Timmerman said.

Connie said, "Why do you get involved with characters that hurt you like this? Can't you stay out of trouble?"

Timmerman said, "Just come as soon as you can."

"I'll come, but it will take some time to collect some supplies. I will be there as soon as I can," she said.

Timmerman hung up grimacing.

Connie entered through the bar's back door, throwing her coat over a chair, and then examining the injury. She removed the bloody towel, wiped the blood away, cauterized, stitched and applied bacitracin. She finally wrapped the finger with a clean bandage. "You have to go to the emergency room," Connie said.

"No, I can't do that. It will get me into more trouble," Timmerman argued.

"You have to go. If infection sets in, it could lead to gangrene," Connie said.

"I'll take my chances."

"You don't understand. If it gets infected, you could lose your hand, or even your arm. I have seen this happen before. If people don't take care of infections, they only get worse," Connie pleaded. "Please listen to me."

"After I settle my score with the Wylies, I'll see a doctor. Until then, I can live on hate," Timmerman said taking a swallow of whiskey.

"Why can't you listen to reason?" Connie begged.

Timmerman said, "I have to take care of business."

Connie left without saying a word, sobbing. Deep down she knew she still loved him. She also knew she couldn't help someone that wouldn't help himself.

Chapter Six

It was Saturday night and that meant karaoke at *Rocky's Bar*. All of us along with our spouses decided to enjoy a night of entertainment. The first few singers were okay, but then the real entertainment started. My wife's good friend, Patti Kane, sang *Mustang Sally*. John and Tyler Baldwin got on stage and sang two of Johnny Cash's all-time favorites, *I Walk the Line* and *Ghost Riders in the Sky*. Carolyn Raft seemed to enjoy Tyler Baldwin's singing. Both songs brought the house down, but the best was yet to come. Ben and Mark sang along to Willie Nelson's and Waylon Jennings' *Good Hearted Woman,* and *Mammas, Don't Let Your Babies Grow Up to be Cowboys.*

Lana Kanton, who does the weather on Channel Seven, stepped up saying she wanted to dedicate her songs to her two good friends, Cindy Mason and Debbie Kinsely. Along with her husband, Max, Lana Kanton sang angelically Karen Carpenter's hits *For All We Know,* and *Yesterday Once More*. When they finished there wasn't a dry eye in the house. Everyone gave them a standing ovation. Even John and Tyler Baldwin had to agree they were great. My wife, Barb, and Patti Kane sang some of Cheryl Crow's best songs including *All I Wanna Do,* and *Leaving Las Vegas*. The rest of the night was pretty wild. We sure know how to enjoy ourselves.

Tom Timmerman came out from his office with his left hand bandaged up. "What happened?" I asked.

"Chain saw," Timmerman answered.

"You should have a doctor look at it before it gets infected," I said.

"I'll think about it," he replied.

When the women were in the bathroom, I asked Tyler Baldwin

if he had heard anything about Debbie Kinsley's murder.

"Yes, we got the report back today. Just like Cindy Mason, she was shot once in the heart. We're still waiting for ballistics, but it will probably take a few days," Tyler said.

Mark said, "It was well known that Cindy Mason liked to have a good time and, according to Debbie Kinsely, Beau was the last person to see her alive. Steve Lemke also dated her before Beau Wylie, giving us two suspects."

When Timmerman stepped into the back alley to dispose of a bag of trash, out of the shadows stepped Steve Lemke. Timmerman was a little startled, thinking Beau Wylie and Jankowski had returned to reinforce their code of silence with the wire cutters, or maybe to make another attempt at getting the cash.

"I'm innocent, Tom Timmerman, and you know it," Steve Lemke whispered.

Timmerman let out a sigh of relief and said, "Lemke, I don't care if you killed that Mason broad, or not. That's your problem. I have enough problems. Keep your friends away from me."

"Listen, it's important that I clear myself. I have been hiding out at Wylie's cottage for days. I know that they're looking for me, but nobody would listen to me if I turn myself in. I'm not going to prison for something I didn't do. I need an alibi for the night of her murder," Steve Lemke demanded.

"What's in it for me?" Tom Timmerman asked.

Lemke stepped toward Timmerman, but thought better if it. Lemke stepped back into the shadows, disappearing into the darkness, heading back toward Wendel Wylie's cottage. As crazy as the Wylies were, he felt safer there since it would be hard for the police to locate him.

The County Courthouse was the center for a swirl of activity. The sheriff's department was under pressure to solve both murders and Carolyn Raft knew she was going to have a busy day. Sheriff Remington had come in early, asking about the Mason and Kinsely autopsies. He wanted some evidence to bring to the district attorney. *The Mining Ledger* was calling for action.

When I dropped in on Carolyn, she half-heartedly grabbed the autopsy utensils, embracing them. I smiled, knowing I had broken the ice with her. I casually asked her, "Is there anything conclusive on the Kinsely case?"

"You would be the last person I would tell. Now leave me alone." Carolyn Raft said.

I could see I had my work cut out ahead of me.

"Now, Carolyn, let's be reasonable. If the case breaks and it's discovered that you helped solve it, you get all the credit. What does it matter who does the grunt work? I want you to get the credit for finding the murderer of those two young women. If something bad happened to you, wouldn't you want my friends to help solve your murder?" I asked, giving her my puppy dog look.

There was total silence in the room. Maybe, I had struck a nerve.

Carolyn said, "How stupid do you think I am? If Sheriff Remington finds out I gave you confidential information, I would be fired and the case could be thrown out. And quit trying to get Tyler in trouble. I have come to think a lot of him and the more time he spends with you, the more likely he will lose his job and his pension. Maybe even be prosecuted for obstruction of justice."

"Carolyn, I will never let that happen," I said. "I don't ask any of my friends to do something I wouldn't do myself. I guess we will just have to make sure Sheriff Remington doesn't find out."

"I should have my head examined," Carolyn said as she handed me the folder, "The report said Debbie Kinsely was shot at close range with the same caliber weapon used to kill Cindy Mason. We found some skin under her fingernails and the murderer's DNA result should be back within days. Whoever did it will have some bad cuts on the left arm and under the left armpit judging from the reenactment we created. The attacker was very strong because Miss Mason had lacerations and bruises from being thrown around."

Carolyn continued, "The deputies also found some cigarettes along the shoreline on the Wylie property. The cigarettes are being examined to see if they turn up any DNA. Judging from the shoe prints, there were two women and a man. It looks like one of the women left, and the other two individuals remained behind. Apparently, the latter two went into the woods. We found meth residue on the ground, so we can assume they must have been smoking. The murderer shot her right in the heart with a .22 caliber. Her death was instantaneous. The killer must have pushed the body into the river, hoping the current would take it downstream. That's when you and your friends saw the body, and retrieved it."

"Now ... I think a bottle of twelve year old Scotch should cover things. And under no circumstances are you to incriminate this office in any way. Do you understand, Mr. Bennett?"

I left the sheriff's office feeling better than I had in a long time.

The station manager, Pete Cotter, left his office at TV 7 every day at six o'clock. Mark and Ben decided to follow him; they both felt he was hiding something. Leaving the station, Cotter stopped outside *Rocky's Bar* to lay a flower alongside the building where Debbie had been found, then headed back to the highway and out the winding county road toward the Dead River. Mark and Ben followed him, easing onto a road overlooking the site where a new cottage was under construction. Cotter left his car, and began pacing back and forth. Wendel Wylie pulled up with his son Beau and Spike Jankowski tagging along.

Sneaking within earshot behind a huge mound of sand dug out of the future basement, Mark and Ben strained to hear their conversation.

Looking at Wendel Wylie, Cotter asked, "Do you know anything about the murders?"

Wendel Wylie replied, "We had absolutely nothing to do with their murders. But I'm not going to waste any tears over them. Mason was starting to probe into my business affairs. I didn't pull out of Detroit and move north to this frozen tundra to get busted by a small time reporter at a tiny TV station. The body would never have been found if I had given the order to kill her. Remember, I tell you the names of the other drug dealers in Mesabi County and you report them to the police. You get your exclusive stories and I get left alone. That was the deal."

Pete Cotter moved toward his car, but Spike Jankowski blocked the car door "There's one more thing. I will take care of any loose ends if they become a problem. Do you hear me?" the senior Wylie threatened.

"Okay, just keep giving me the info and I'll stay out of this mess," Cotter responded.

"There's one more thing, Cotter. I don't want any more reporters poking around my place. Do you understand?" Wendel barked.

Pete Cotter said, "Yes, I understand." He realized that he had challenged the wrong people.

Mark and Ben heard only some of the conversation, but just that Cotter had taken it upon himself to meet the three thugs added another piece to the puzzle. And they both desperately needed to solve this thing: It might have been their conversations with Debbie Kinsely that led to her death.

Monday night was team meeting night at *Geno's Pizzeria.* Rick Bonnettelli made us feel welcome, served up the beer and pizza, and we reviewed what we knew.

"We know both victims were shot with a .22 caliber handgun at close range and in cold blood, and then discarded like garbage in the river, or in the alley," I said. I also shared the details that Carolyn had traded for a bottle of twelve-year old Scotch.

Mark summed it up: "The police found three sets of footprints. The two women were probably Cindy Mason and Debbie Kinsely. So who was the man?"

"Well… there's Timmerman… I'm not so sure that he tangled with a chain saw. I'll keep an eye on him," John Baldwin said.

"And what about Lemke?" He's wanted by the Needleton Police for questioning in the first murder, but seems to have disappeared. That seems to suggest he's got something to hide,"

Tyler Baldwin said.

"Let's check on Jack Cannon's background. He seemed like he was hiding something," Ben added.

"And there is the Wylie crew," Mark pointed out. "I don't think it could have been Wendel, but we should keep Beau and Jankowski on the short list."

"They can usually be found at the cottage next door. I can cast an eye that way from time to time. For now, how about if I follow Jack Cannon?" I proposed.

We didn't see much of one another over the next few days. On Thursday, we met at Millie's Restaurant in Victorious. All we had to report was that the five suspects –- Timmerman, Lemke, Cannon, Beau Wylie and Spike Jankowski – were either AWOL or unpredictable.

Another week passed. By mid-December, winter had settled in, temperatures dropped well below freezing every day and sometimes near 0° overnight. Snowmobilers could be heard in the distance racing up and down the frozen river and cross country skiers and snowshoers passed by near our cottage. Local residents, Kenny and Megan Bievins, were snow-shoeing toward the dam and stopped at our cabin for refreshments.

"Any word on the murders?" Kenny Bievins asked.

"No, the trail is as cold as the river." I replied, "But we're still working the case.

"I hope someone catches them soon. I hate to think there could be cold blooded killers among us," Megan Bievins said as she tied her straps and they snow shoed off.

That got me thinking. Maybe, we had been working the case the wrong way. We were trying to find out where they had been and whom they were with. Maybe it was time to turn it around and focus on why they were killed. The team agreed: We had to find out why Cindy Mason's and Debbie Kinsley's bodies were found in their respective locations.

Tyler and John Baldwin returned to *Rocky's* alley to see if they could find anything incriminating that had been overlooked, admittedly a long shot at this late date. Mark, Ben and I walked along the shoreline of the Dead River, hoping to find something that belonged to Cindy Mason.

As we approached Turtle Island, we noticed something floating in the open water, surrounded by ice floes. Mark looked through his binoculars and reported, "It looks like part of a life jacket, or a backpack or purse of some kind."

The dilemma was how to retrieve it without falling thorough the ice. Ben suggested that we form a human chain. After returning from his truck, Ben handed us a safety rope which we attached to our waists, and then we crawled across the ice toward the open water. Since I was the heaviest, I laid down first, nearest the shore. Ben lay closer and Mark lay closest to the open water.

We crept toward the open water, expecting at any minute to fall through. When Mark approached the edge, Ben handed him a tree branch. Mark hooked onto the object, which was, in fact, a purse, pulling it toward him. Slowly, we crawled toward the beach.

"Whose is it?" Mark asked.

"It's Cindy Mason's," Ben said. "And there's a bunch of papers all matted together at the bottom. Let's take these back to your cottage, Bill, and see if Barb can get them apart."

After an hour of careful work, Barb had indeed separated the various receipts, grocery lists and other papers as best she could. The printing on many was completely gone. On several, the ink had bled, but some the handwritten message was still legible. Ben tried to piece it, together out loud.

> *Ja... ... Deb..., ... late to Wylie's cottage.   ....*
> *check .... facts. ...... the Wylies ... in Detroit. ....*
> *warrants against them.*
> *Cindy*

"Wow. So the third set of footprints belonged to Jack Cannon and Cindy really was on some kind of a mission, but didn't leave her message to the others before joining them at Wylie's cottage," Mark said.

Ben agreed, "I'll deliver all of this to the sheriff's office tomorrow. Let's call it a night."

Chapter Seven

As I was driving onto the Camp Road the next morning, I noticed something shimmering in the woods in a little clearing a few hundred feet down a logging road. Stopping to investigate, I noticed the litter pile that was starting to accumulate and muttered to myself about neighbors who wouldn't pay the private garbage disposal service to handle their trash. When I noticed jars, coolers, propane tanks, starting fluid containers, acetone cans, smashed batteries, and plastic bottles, my old police instincts came back. The torn up bills addressed to Wendel Wylie in the decomposing garbage bag added another piece to the puzzle. I called my comrades.

Strolling cautiously among the debris, John confirmed my suspicions that someone had been cooking crystal meth and using this area as their dump site. We called Sherriff Remington, who called for a search warrant. On our way back to my cottage, so as not to attract suspicion, or further disturb the site, we observed the Wylie's cottage with a look of disgust.

Deputy Roads arrived with the search warrant and several members of the State Hazardous Removal Team arrived, Sheriff Remington explained the plan: "Deputy Roads and I will knock on the Wylie's front door; the rest of you should head down by the river in case they try to escape that way. Once we have them rounded up, the state hazardous unit can start investigating the dump site." It sounded like a good plan.

Sheriff Remington and Deputy Roads knocked on the cottage door, shouting "Mesabi County Sheriff". We heard banging and crashing inside the building, and then a tremendous blast took out all the doors and windows, blowing the sheriff and the deputy backwards and engulfing the cottage in flames. The fireball rose several hundred feet into the air. Tyler and John attended to the sheriff and deputy until the paramedics arrived.

The emergency responders treated both Sheriff Remington and Deputy Roads for what appeared to be third-degree burns, and then loaded them into ambulances and sped away. Shortly, the Needleton Township Fire Department arrived, although there was little that could be done, and given the deep snow, there was no need to worry that the fire would spread. From the heat of the fire, they speculated that a meth lab had exploded.

Hours later, the firemen located two bodies, both were burned beyond recognition. When Carolyn Raft arrived, Tyler approached her, but she motioned for him to stay away. After examining the bodies, they were placed in bags and taken away.

"What do you think, Carolyn? Are there any early guesses?" Tyler asked.

"Not much," she said, "Two males. One is middle-aged and the other one is in his twenties. The younger one was probably about six feet tall. The older man was shorter with a dental bridge in his lower jaw. The State Fire Marshall will examine the debris and take samples tomorrow. I'll have more information on the victims in a few days."

Tyler thanked her, and then returned to share the news with the rest of us.

Chapter Eight

From his hiding place up in the woods not far from the ashes of Wylie's cottage, Tom Timmerman smiled. Just before the sheriff and his deputy knocked on the cottage door, he had thrown a Molotov cocktail through the back window, crawling away on his hands and knees and smirking about how he had gotten even with the men who had severed part of his finger. With a last look of satisfaction, he drove off – he could always find a new supplier, and now he wouldn't have to pay the Wylies anything. More importantly, he'd gotten his revenge, and in a spectacular way at that

Following up on their self-assigned task – to watch Pete Cotter – Mark and Ben watched the television station well past Cotter's normal quitting time, then entered and asked the new receptionist if Cotter was there. She looked up and said, "No, Mr. Cotter has not been in all day. We're not sure where he is."

Tyler didn't have any better luck finding Steve Lemke. Entering *Rocky's Bar,* he approached Tom Timmerman, who was talking to his ex-wife Connie.

"Have you seen Steve Lemke?" Tyler asked.

"Yeah. Last Saturday night. He had a few drinks."

"Know where he might be?" Tyler Baldwin asked.

"No, I can't say as I can," Tom Timmerman replied.

Tyler Baldwin looked at Timmerman and said, "If he comes back, be sure to call me at the station."

Timmerman looked at Tyler smugly and said, "Sure thing, Sargent Baldwin."

I drove past Jack Cannon's place. He was renting an apartment in an old Victorian home near the Victorious library. It was once a very distinguished and exclusive part of town, but wasn't as well maintained as it could have been and some folks rented out rooms to help defray expenses. Cannon's black Corvette was parked under the carport. Darkness comes early in the winter to the Superior Peninsula and in the dim light; I saw two silhouettes enter the apartment from the side door. The lights came on upstairs. Shadows moved back and forth. Suddenly, a window was thrown open and a body was thrown out. It was Jack Cannon, moaning and barely alive. I called 911, and then two shadows ran down the steps and through the bushes, speeding away down the alley in what looked like an older pickup truck. I called John. He said he would call the others.

A Victorious police cruiser pulled up and a young patrolman stepped out and identified himself as Officer Burns. The young officer glanced at the window as he nodded and took my statement. The EMTs tended to Cannon, then he was whisked away to the ER. Officer Burns took the home owners' statements and the forensics team searched the apartment. I was pretty sure it wouldn't be much help.

"I wonder what the attempted murderers were looking for," Mark said.

"He must have known something. Nobody throws a person out a window without a reason," Ben offered, as we scanned the area with flashlights, hoping to find any clue at all.

"Over here," John called. It was a DVD. Officer Burns slid on a pair of latex gloves, picked up the DVD, and placed it into an evidence bag. Our continued search turned up nothing else.

We adjourned to *Geno's Pizzeria* for beer and pizza and downed the first two pitchers with ease.

"I bet that DVD has nothing to do with the case; some kid probably threw it Frisbee-style and it landed in the yard," Ben proposed.

"It all depends on what's on the DVD. Someone could have given it to John for safe keeping," Tyler Baldwin continued, "Dad and I can check on Jack Cannon."

"Well, it looks like Jack Cannon had something on the murderers and they wanted him out of the picture," John said.

Ben and I decided to meet the next morning at the Victorious police station. We had nothing to lose and, maybe, we could smooth talk our way into viewing the DVD.

Chapter Nine

We entered the Victorious police station, carrying a box of donuts from *The Mountain Fresh Bakery*. A box of deep-fried, sugary bribery had been known to work in the past. Officer Burns looked up, eying the box of donuts.

"Hello, Officer Burns," I said cheerfully.

"Can I help you?" he asked.

"Well, maybe, you can. Do you think we could get a peek at the DVD?" Ben Myers asked.

"Afraid I can't do that," he retorted.

"You won't help a couple of old law enforcement officers in their golden years?" I asked.

"Not even if I could," Officer Burns replied. "The DVD was sent to the lab for fingerprinting."

"Do you mean it is at the Mesabi County Sheriff's Department?" Ben asked.

"Yes, that's correct," Officer Burns replied.

"Thanks," we replied.

"What about the donuts?" Officer Burns asked.

It was a short ride over to the Sheriffs' Department. On the way, we picked up Tyler, thinking that he would be an asset in persuading Carolyn Raft to help us out. We ducked down the back stairs and quietly opened her lab door.

"Get out, and take your friends with you," Carolyn stated.

"Hello, Carolyn, this is Ben Myers. He's a retired officer from the Victorious Police Department and you already know Tyler. They're both as close to legal as one can get. How about if you allow us to watch the DVD that was recovered last night?" I asked. "After all, it was our team that found it."

"Listen, I'm in enough trouble already because of you. There is no way I'm going upstairs and take that DVD," she said.

"I understand, but I thought you cared about Sheriff Remington and Deputy Roads. You know that they've been transferred to the burn unit in Milwaukee, right?"

She left the room, returned, and handed me the DVD.

"There's a DVD player over there between the Centrifuse Rotary Evaporator and the Calorimeter," Carolyn said with a smirk.

"In English," I responded.

"On the left side, half-way down," Carolyn said condescendingly.

I located the monitor, put latex gloves on, and slid the DVD into the player. We all leaned forward as the picture gradually emerged on the screen. There stood Cindy Mason, staring at the camera holding a microphone.

"Hello, this is Cindy Mason broadcasting from the site of a meth lab. The building behind me belongs to Wendel Wylie and his son Beau. To my shame, I have bought meth from my supplier, Tom Timmerman, who purchases it from these people. I know this will be the end of my career, but the truth has to come out and I am ready to face the consequences. This is Cindy Mason signing off for the last time." The screen went blank.

We couldn't take our eyes off the monitor. Carolyn finally reached over pressing the eject button. Wearing latex gloves, she removed the DVD from the player, sliding it back into the evidence bag.

"That's unbelievable," Carolyn said.

It was a hollow victory. We had seen what we wanted to see, but we still didn't know who killed her. The evidence certainly pointed toward the Wylies, but they were dead, right? If not, who were the two bodies in Wylie's cottage? How did Jack Cannon end up with the DVD anyway? And whose DNA was under Cindy Mason's fingernails? We had a lot of work to do.

Chapter Ten

John and his son Tyler entered the Victorious Hospital. They were going to try to obtain information from Jack Cannon. They approached the charge nurse and asked, "Excuse me. Could you tell us if Jack Cannon can see visitors?"

"He is heavily sedated and, no, he cannot see anyone," the charge nurse replied.

"Thank you," John said.

Pretending to leave the reception area, they paused, waiting for the charge nurse to move out of view, and then walked toward the patients' rooms, glancing in each room as they passed. Halfway down the hallway, they found Cannon lying in a bed, an IV in one arm and both legs heavily bandaged.

"Jack, Jack Cannon, can you hear me?" He whispered.

Jack Cannon moaned, "Get the DVD."

"What's on the DVD?" John asked ever so softly.

"Everything," Jack Cannon said under his breath.

"Who attacked you?" Tyler asked.

"Wendel and Beau Wylie," Jack Cannon said barely conscious.

"Who are you and what are you doing here? the charge nurse bellowed. "Get out. Now."

We reconvened at *Millie's Restaurant* and exchanged information. It appeared that both Steve Lemke and Pete Cotter were missing. I told the others about Cindy Mason's DVD; the Baldwins told us about Jack Cannon's tip regarding his attackers. Now we had to wait until the report came back identifying the DNA found under Cindy Mason's fingernails. We also had to find out if the two bodies found in the rubble were indeed Wendel and Beau Wylie. Was Jack Cannon believable? Could Wendel and Beau Wylie actually be alive?

Chapter Eleven

That evening Carolyn Raft's phone rang.

"How are you doing? Would you like to have a drink tonight at *Reflections*?" Tyler asked.

She didn't want to appear too eager. "Well, I have to work tomorrow."

"Maybe, a night out might do you some good," he replied sympathetically.

"Well, maybe one drink." Pick me up at 9:00?"

Carolyn was examining her hair and make-up one last time prior to the arrival of her prospective knight in shining armor when the doorbell rang. Smiling, she opened the door. But the smile turned into a look of horror: it wasn't Tyler after all. Someone in a dark hooded sweatshirt threw a blinding liquid in her face. As the hooded attacker was lighting a match, the attacker's arm was grabbed from behind and the attacker fell backward, away from her door. The two men tumbled down the steps together, and then the hooded stranger stood up, running away from the building into the darkness.

Tyler stumbled to his knees. His first thought was to help Carolyn. he fell through the door, putting his arms around Carolyn and leading her into the kitchen. He grabbed a towel, helping her to wipe the liquid from her face. The distinctive odor told him that the substance was gasoline. "Let's get you into the shower."

She pointed toward the second floor. He helped her up the stairs and into the bathroom, turned on the shower, and closed the door. "I'll call this into the station," he said.

"This is Sargent Baldwin. I want to report a 245 in progress at 145 Case Street. Suspect is at large," he said. "Someone threw gasoline in Carolyn's face and was about to throw a match on her when I grabbed the perp's arm from behind. The attacker ran off. I didn't get a good look at him, but he was wearing a black hooded sweatshirt."

Officer Dalrymple arrived at the house while other officers dispersed through the neighborhood, knocking on doors. Nobody had seen, or heard anything. Carolyn came down dressed in a bathrobe, and visibly shaken. She started weeping when she looked at the doorway. She was furious at herself. Thinking that it was Tyler, she opened the door without asking who it was. She could have been killed. Who would want to hurt her? She had never done anything to anyone.

Carolyn went upstairs to bed and Tyler spent the night on the couch. Officer Dalrymple parked his cruiser in front of her house. In spite of her worries, Carolyn smiled the next morning when she came downstairs, seeing Tyler lying with his feet over the end of the couch. She covered him up with a blanket and made a pot of coffee.

That night, Timmerman had parked his car two blocks away from Carolyn's house. When the attack failed, he quietly retraced his steps and returned to his bar in Needleton. He had only been gone about 20 minutes. He hoped that his plan to confuse the police would give them something to think about for a while. It would give him time to take over the meth manufacturing. With the Wylies out of the way, he could now use Lemke and Jankowski as his pawns. Timmerman sure didn't want the police nosing around his bar while he moved up in the world.

Chapter Twelve

"Rocky's Bar," Timmerman answered when the phone rang. Silence, then a voice asked, "You didn't think you could get rid of me that easy, did you Timmerman?" Timmerman held his breath.

"Hello, who is this?" Timmerman asked, pretending to be innocent.

"You know damn well who this is. You are a rotten bastard. I'm going to get you if it's the last thing I do," Wendel Wylie threatened.

The phone went dead.

Timmerman tried to compose himself: They had to be dead. There's no way anyone could have survived that blast. *The Mining Ledger* had reported that there were two bodies found in the debris. They couldn't have survived.

Leaving the bar one more time, Timmerman hurried home, scurried into his basement and retrieved his 9 mm pistol, making sure it was loaded. If anybody came after him, he would be ready. He filled a water glass with the hard stuff from his liquor cabinet, and then consumed it in seconds. He needed reinforcement.

"Hello," said the voice on the other end.

"Lemke, is that you?" Tom Timmerman asked. "You told me a few days ago you needed an alibi the night Cindy Mason was murdered. Do you still want one?"

"Yes. It's time for me to get back into circulation now that the Wylie cottage is gone."

"It's going to cost you," Tom Timmerman responded. "I need some help taking care of your friends," Tom Timmerman said.

"Not a chance. They're crazy. If they think I helped you, they'll come after me," Steve Lemke said.

"The way I see it, you don't have a choice. Help me out, or the police will pin the Mason and Kinsely murder raps on you," Timmerman answered.

After a long silence, Lemke reluctantly responded. "What do you want me to do?"

"Meet me in one hour at my bar," Tom Timmerman said.

When Lemke arrived at *Rocky's Bar*, it was empty except for Timmerman. He was sitting at a table drinking whiskey. Lemke pulled up a chair. After a long pause, Lemke summoned the courage to say, "Do you have a plan? You don't even know where they are hiding, do you?"

Tom Timmerman glared at Steve Lemke and said, "I know where they're hiding. There's an old furniture store warehouse near the entrance into town. The store's been abandoned, and they store their meth in the back."

Lemke had been with Beau and Spike to drop off the meth. He nodded in approval and said, "You're probably right, but what do you want to do?"

"You and I are going to pay them a visit later tonight. They don't think I know about their warehouse. Cindy Mason told me. She was with Beau when he dropped off a shipment. Cindy was a good investigator. So good that it got her killed," Timmerman said without emotion.

Steve Lemke went over to the bar, taking a glass from behind. He returned to the table, putting the glass in front of Timmerman. He proceeded to fill it to the top and said, "We're going to need a little liquid courage for this project, aren't we?" Lemke drained his glass.

The two sat in silence for several hours, sipping their drinks and staring at the wall. When the clock struck twelve, Tom Timmerman stood up. It took Steve Lemke several attempts just to get his balance. Timmerman handed his 9 mm pistol to Lemke, and then took a twelve gauge shotgun out of the broom closet. He smiled at Lemke, leading him through the doorway into the dark alley.

Wendel Wylie sat on an old couch in the abandoned furniture

store. Beau Wylie sat staring out the window thinking that he'd had it pretty great just a week ago: He was making a lot of money manufacturing meth and dating the most beautiful woman in the county. Since she needed meth to function, she was beholden to him for life. Then suddenly, it all came crashing down. Someone had killed her. Tom Timmerman threw a homemade bomb through the cottage window in an attempt to kill them. Dumping the meth waste on that logging road near their cottage had clearly been a bad idea. He had heard that two bodies were found in the carnage and knew that Spike was probably one of them. His buddy Spike would be alive now if they had just followed orders.

Beau Wylie asked, "We were lucky weren't we, Pa?"

"What do you mean?" Wendel Wylie asked.

"We could have been killed in the cottage if we'd got back five minutes earlier. It's good we saw the sheriff and his deputy parking their cars next door. Timmerman's Molotov Cocktail would have killed us for sure. And to see that snake creeping away from the building, thinking that he'd done us good."

"Yeah, I guess you're right, son. If we had been a littler earlier we would have been blown to Hell," Wendel Wyllie said.

The Wylies had been hiding in the warehouse ever since. They cleaned their pistols and were going to go to *Rocky's* and kill Tom Timmerman when the bar closed that night.

Beau nudged his father's leg, waking him up at the sound of activity at the back door to the warehouse. His son motioned for him to be silent, pointing toward the back door. Thinking it might be the police, the Wylies crouched behind some of the moth-eaten furniture. They could hear footsteps, and then saw Timmerman's shotgun pointed their way. Gunfire erupted. Timmerman stood straight up for a minute, and then fell face down.

"Whoever you are drop your gun, or you'll end up like Timmerman," Wendel Wylie shouted.

A 9 mm was tossed over the furniture and Lemke screamed from the doorway, "It wasn't my idea. Timmerman made me come. He was the only person who could give me an alibi for Cindy's murder."

Wendel walked toward Steve Lemke, raised his pistol and pulled the trigger. Lemke fell over on his side.

Wendel looked at Beau Wylie and said, "Let that be a lesson to you, son. Don't trust anybody that isn't family."

They dragged the bodies behind the couches, loaded up the meth in the back of their pickup, shut the warehouse door, and headed for Lemke's house in Victorious. "You know that no one will be home," Wendel chortled.

Chapter Thirteen

Since Timmerman had not been seen in a few days, Tyler had begun watching Steve Lemke's house as time permitted. Late that night, a truck pulled into the driveway. The passenger stepped out and soon the garage door opened. The truck proceeded inside and the door closed behind it. The lights went on inside the garage and Tyler could hear some bumps and thuds coming from within.

Tyler called for backup from the Victorious Police Dispatcher, but there had been a truck/automobile accident at the new round-a-bout and everyone had been dispatched to help out at the scene of the accident.

Tyler called his father. John said he would be there in minutes and would contact Mark, Ben and me. Minutes later, Tyler Baldwin was glad to see us. Tyler did not have authorization since he was not a Victorious police officer to act, but until the accident was cleared up on the highway, there would be no support. It definitely was a *Catch 22.*

We spread out around the perimeter of the house, and then heard the truck start inside the garage. Diving behind trees, bushes, fences, and anything that could provide cover, we looked like the Keystone Cops from decades ago. But it worked; the truck backed out of the garage; someone closed the garage door and climbed into the passenger seat. As the truck sped off, Tyler and his dad followed, but we had seen enough. In the few moments that it took to close the door, we observed the results of the Wylie's labor. We called in our report. When Officer Burns arrived, he told us to stand aside; he'd call use when it was acceptable to join him. He also reminded us that anything suspicious had to be in plain sight. He approached the side door and knocked. We knew protocol had to be followed. He shouted, "Victorious police and I have a search warrant for the premises." There was no reply. He promptly kicked the door in, turned the lights on and opened the garage door. Meth bags were piled to the ceiling. "I think that qualifies as plain sight," I said. Even though we couldn't enter, we could enjoy the personal reward of having been on the scene when the cache of crystal meth was recovered.

Within minutes, several other cruisers arrived, each gaping at the sheer amount. The street value would have been in the hundreds of thousands. We helped the officers squeeze it all into the police van.

While all of this was happening in Lemke's garage, Tyler and John had followed the black truck, out along the narrow and dangerous county road that led out toward the Dead River. When the truck proceeded off the blacktop onto a gravel road, the Baldwins called it quits. No way would there ever be two vehicles out this way at night in the dead of winter. The Baldwins knew they would be easily seen and tip off the unknown thugs. As they retraced their route, John's phone rang. "No kidding!" he said. He disconnected and said to Tyler "You were right. The crooks loaded Lemke's garage with meth. They barely fit everything in the police van."

Holed up in their car in a plow-out along the side of the road, Beau complained, "How long do you want to stay in this place?"

Wendel said, "We'll stay here overnight and move on tomorrow. When things quiet down, we'll go back and move our stash to Wisconsin. We'll be all right because we're smart. We know when to pull out."

They were, however, totally unaware that their meth was being delivered at that very minute to the Mesabi County Sherriff's Office. Federal drug agents were on their way to Victorious to take custody.

The next morning, Ben Myers called, "I just heard from a buddy that Cindy Mason's DNA report has come back."

I phoned Tyler and said, "Do you want to come with me to see

Carolyn? We need to ascertain the results of the DNA."

"Sure, I can come." Once again, I thought he had an ulterior motive.

Arriving at Carolyn's lab, Tyler smiled and motioned for me to stay back.

"Hello, Carolyn! Everything okay? How about if I come over tonight? I could bring some wine and we could watch a movie," Tyler said.

"Maybe, but you didn't come all the way down here to ask me for a date. What do you really want?" Carolyn asked.

"Could you tell us about the DNA report?" Tyler asked.

"Well, it would help a lot towards finding the killer of Cindy Mason and Debbie Kinsely," I said.

She glared at me. "This is your idea isn't it?" she said. I felt like a kid with his hand in the cookie jar.

"Carolyn, it would mean a lot to me if you could help us," Tyler murmured.

She said, "I'll check it out."

All she found out from the guy in Forensics was that the DNA evidence didn't have a match in the system. This meant the accused did not have a criminal record, which pretty much ruled out the Wylies and Spike Jankowski.

Before we left, Tyler gave her a hug and a peck on the cheek. I moved toward her and she said, "Don't even think it."

Chapter Fourteen

After the Christmas and New Year's holidays, the long cold winter had really set in. It was time to catch up on our least favorite chores. My hunting clothes needed to be washed, and I oiled and cleaned my Remington .308. As a last task, I sat down to delete the old video footage from my trail cams. Each one held eleven minutes of recordings on the chip, which was plenty since the cameras only clicked on in response to movement. Reliving the hunting season one last time, I decided to enjoy the footage. I put the chip in my laptop, sitting back to enjoy. A beautiful doe and her fawn wandered down the trail, the fawn was leading the way, totally unaware of its surroundings and the doe following a minute later ever so cautiously, her ears rotating, listening for danger.

Twice the doe stopped, smelling the air; then, something provoked her. She snorted and bounded out of the picture. Just a few seconds of recording time remained and I was about to eject the chip, when I saw motion in the distance. It was a person running through the woods, then coming toward the camera following the deer trail. It looked like Cindy Mason; a man wearing a baseball cap came into view, aiming a pistol at her. She ran in front of the camera, tripped, fell, and then struggled with the man, who slapped her across the face. As the last few seconds of the recording ticked down, I saw her struggle, but he got the upper hand, raised his pistol and fired

I had to show the others immediately. I called John.

"John. I was cleaning up my trail cam footage and you've got to see this," I said.

"Not another deer story," he replied, clearly annoyed.

"No. I saw Cindy Mason. Call your son and I'll call Mark and

Ben."

Once the team was assembled, I inserted the chip. Everyone smiled when the fawn and doe worked their way down the trail, and then dashed out of view. The picture changed. We saw Cindy Mason running for her life. We couldn't believe our eyes.

"We're going to have to get the video enhanced," Ben said.

"Yes, and we can let the police take it from there," Mark said.

With the video chip in hand, we sped to the Mesabi County Sheriff Department. Carolyn was reviewing some papers with a forensic technician. She looked at us and said, "No, don't even think it; I don't ever want to see you in here again." She started to walk away.

"Well, do you want to see Cindy Mason's murderer?" I asked.

"What do you mean?" she asked.

"I have it all on my trail cam, but we can't make out the assassin's face. It has to be enhanced. Do you know anyone who could do that?" I asked.

"Give me the chip," she demanded.

Walking fast, she went up a flight of stairs with us on her heels. Carolyn opened the *Forensics* lab door and approached a geeky looking guy who she introduced as Dan. She whispered into his ear and smiled. She could be very charming when she wanted to. He walked over to a monitor and inserted the chip. Before long, the deer appeared on the monitor. Then Cindy Mason could be seen running toward the camera, followed by her murderer.

Don enhanced the image of the murderer's face   coming into focus was the face of the murderer. It was Cindy's colleague from the station, sports-caster Jack Cannon. My jaw dropped. He was the last one I suspected. Pressing a few buttons, he printed an 8" x 10" glossy of Cindy's murderer. We walked across the hall to the sheriff's office. With the sheriff and Deputy Roads still undergoing plastic surgery in Milwaukee, we learned that Sergeant Phil Benton was in charge. "How's retirement treating you? Can I help you?" he asked.

"Phil, I think we're the ones who can help you. I caught Cindy Mason's murderer on my trail cam and here's the picture. The forensics guy, Don, just reproduced it across the hall." Phil Benton was still skeptical. With us following right behind, he marched over to the forensics lab, where once again Don inserted the chip, and we watched the doe and fawn come down the trail, followed by the murder scene. "Thanks for the evidence, boys. We'll take over now. Jack Cannon is still in the rehab facility, so we know where to find him."

Chapter Fifteen

Carolyn joined us for beer and pizza at *Geno's Pizzeria* that night. She squeezed into the booth next to Tyler, greeted Ben and shook hands with Mark and told John that she understood where Tyler got his good looks. I told her Tyler's good looks came from his mother." She just squinted at me. It was nice to be appreciated.

Since we seemed to pretty much have the first murder wrapped up, we sorted through the remaining suspects in the second one. Interestingly, nobody had seen Pete Cotter, Tom Timmerman, or Steve Lemke for days. And what about the two bodies in the Wylie cottage? Carolyn lowered her voice. "Actually, I have some information, but you would have to promise to keep it to yourselves. The fire at Wylie's cottage wasn't started by the meth lab. The State Fire Marshall found an incendiary device that triggered the explosion and then ignited the meth chemicals in a chain reaction. Also, about the bodies ... it was Spike Jankowski and Pete Cotter."

"Why didn't you tell us earlier today?" I asked.

"Why didn't you ask?" she replied smiling.

Sometimes, I think she just liked to aggravate me.

Everyone started speaking simultaneously.

"One person at a time now," I said, "Ben, why don't you start?"

"That means the Wylies are still out there. They must be hiding out waiting to retrieve their goods," he said.

"Exactly," Tyler added. "We can stake out Steve Lemke's garage. They don't know we have their stuff."

"Good idea. Much better than trying to turn the county upside down to find them," I said.

John, Tyler and I took the first watch. Just before the sun rose, both John and Tyler were asleep in the front of the vehicle. In the back seat, I was on my third cup of coffee.

A truck approached, and then passed by. I leaned forward to nudge both of them awake. Watching the action in the outside passenger mirror, we saw the truck turn around and pull into the driveway. The passenger got out and entered the garage through the side door; the main door rose slowly, turning the light on. Several minutes of angry gestures, pointed fingers, and swearing followed. They were enraged.

Tyler dialed 911. "This is Needleton Sergeant Baldwin. I need back-up at 315 Waldorf Street. There is a 211 in progress. Burglars are presumed armed and dangerous. Send back-up ASAP."

While Tyler was calling, the two men closed the garage door and got back into their truck. John suddenly started his engine, crept forward, then veered at the last minute, smashing his truck into the front of theirs. They were pinned by the garage in front and our vehicle behind. They jumped out shooting. We returned fire. In the distance we heard police sirens. That was music to our ears. We just wanted to keep them pinned down until help arrived.

Hearing the sirens, the Wylies ran for the woods. John shot Wendel in the leg; catching up, he pushed Wendel Wylie's face to the ground and held him until Ben arrived. Beau Wylie ran behind the garage. Tyler and I gave pursuit. As fast as Beau was, Tyler was even faster. When Beau tried to take aim, Tyler kicked the gun out of his hand. Tyler handcuffed him and pulled him to his feet. By the time I arrived, it was over.

"Nice going," I said to Tyler gasping for breath.

Officer Dalrymple read them their rights and held them behind the squad car. Once the paramedics arrived, they cleaned and bandaged Wendel Wylie's leg wound, then whisked him off to Victorious Hospital. Officer Dalrymple rode along in the ambulance.

The next morning we reconvened at the Sheriff's Office.

The Wylies had talked, telling police that they would find Tom Timmerman's and Steve Lemke's bodies in the abandoned furniture warehouse. Jack Cannon talked, too: he admitted to the murders of both Cindy Mason and Debbie Kinsely. Thanks to Cindy's investigation, Jack Cannon knew that people would find out that he, Cindy and Debbie were using meth. He also knew that nobody would hire a drug-addicted sports announcer. His dream of moving up the ladder to a national sports network would be shattered. Cannon pleaded with Cindy not to go public, but she wouldn't be deterred. He watched while she made the incriminating video of the Wylie's drug operation at the cottage. When reasoning with her, hoping he could change her mind before she brought it back to the television station, failed, he showed Cindy his .22. She dashed off into the woods with Cannon giving chase, right into view of my video trail cam. Although it wasn't shown on video, Cannon admitted to dragging her body to the Dead River, hoping the current would take it down to the dam. Cannon didn't count on low winter water levels, or there being a sand bar.

As for the bodies in the meth lab, Cindy Mason had told Jack Cannon days earlier that Pete Cotter was getting inside information from Wylie regarding the drug dealers in the area. Cotter must have decided to return to Wylie's cottage at exactly the wrong moment. He and Spike Jankowski were in the cottage when it blew up.

When it appeared that Debbie Kinsely was going to crack under the strain, Jack Cannon decided that he had to kill her, too. He lured her into the alley with a promise that he would confront Timmerman. After all, it was Timmerman who got them hooked on meth in the first place. He also hoped that killing Debbie outside of *Rocky's Bar* would incriminate Timmerman. Driving away unnoticed, using a throw-away phone, he called in the crime himself.

Chapter Sixteen

The next day, we assembled once again at *Geno's Pizzeria*. Even Carolyn was there. We toasted our investigative accomplishments and thanked her for sharing critical information. She sat next to Tyler; they seemed to be getting along nicely.

She also reported that Sergeant Benton had found Cindy Mason's journal in the glove compartment of Jack Cannon's Corvette. Nobody ever said murderers were smart. With the added evidence, the trial would be a slam dunk. Everything was there – the dates when she, Debbie Kinsely and Jack Cannon had purchased meth from Timmerman, the location of the lab and her visits with Beau Wylie to the furniture warehouse. Evidence from the trail cam sealed the case. Carolyn also let us know that Sheriff Remington and Deputy Roads were back home in Victorious, completing physical therapy at the local hospital.

The next day, I decided to pay Sheriff Remington a visit. His wife opened the door. "Strom might be a little irritable, but he will still be glad to see you," she said.

"Strom, how are you doing?" I asked

"I've been better," said Sheriff Remington. "They had to do skin grafts, and it will take time to recover. I heard your crew helped solve the murders. I can't understand how you got enough information to continue the investigation," he said with a smile.

"I guess we're just good detectives." I replied, trying to look innocent.

"You're just lucky I wasn't around. I would have thrown all five of you in the clink for obstruction of justice, withholding evidence, breaking and entering, loitering, and any other crimes I could think of," snorted Sheriff Remington.

"Strom, your department came out looking great." I smiled, trying to put a good face on it.

"You wait until I get back to my office. Your days of running roughshod over legal procedures are done. There's a reason why information is kept private. Now get out of here. I don't want to see you, or your crew flaunting the law again." The smile on his face tempered his rough words.

As I walked to the door, Strom's wife hugged me. "Strom acts like an old bear. He pretends to be cranky, but he thinks the world of you. We'll always appreciate what you and your friends did. She gave me a hug. "And thanks for coming; he'd love a visit any time and I wouldn't mind having him out of my hair for an hour or two!" she said. That was worth a million bucks. I said, "We all worked together to solve the *deer trail murders*."

Part III

Fireworks on the Dead River

Chapter One

Summer in the Superior Peninsula was the most glorious time of the year. It had been a long and cold winter, but the deep snowdrifts and shoveling were a thing of the past, at least for now. As May and June unfolded, the sun rose farther to the north every day. At the summer solstice, it would stay light until at least 10:00 p.m. Mesabi County was coming alive again. Like the snowbirds who left Mesabi county each winter, the robins were back, prowling about our yard looking for earthworms. Turtles liked to crawl up onto our beach, enjoying the sunshine. If you walked near them, though, they quickly disappeared into the river. The deer came to drink at the river's edge; they were almost tame. Squirrels scurried from tree to tree. The wild cherries were in full bloom and the lush green foliage gave everything a fresh smell. Flowers were starting to burst open and bees zoomed from blossom to blossom.

It was a wonderful time to listen to the sounds of life. On that beautiful sunny morning, my wife, Barb, and I were doing that. As we walked along the beach, we could hear cars arriving and the sounds of hammers and saws. To me the nicest sound of all was children's laughter as they played on the beach and in the shallow water.

We were thankful to be living in one of the most beautiful areas of the country. The whole experience on the Dead River is wonderful. I had no responsibilities – I was retired and free to do what I wanted every day, perhaps going for a boat ride, or getting down and dirty in the mud on a bike ride with "the band of brothers in mud and blood." Or maybe, fishing, or visiting a neighbor. Over the years, I had made some great friends and it was fun to drop in on them to catch up on the news. The only real problems of the day might be whether, or not the fish were biting, or if the water was warms enough to swim. After a frantic and stressful career as the sheriff of Victorious, Michigan, I was finally learning to slow down and enjoy everything around me. I really loved to go out on the river in the morning, fishing from my kayak before the boat traffic became too heavy. I must confess that sometimes I found it so peaceful that I forgot what I was doing. Enjoying the beauty of nature caused me to miss a few fish.

Almost four hundred fellow land-owners shared the same love for the Dead River. Ken and Betty Durant had raised their daughter, Jenni, while living on the river. Jenni was a beautiful, independent, young woman who loved adventure. As a child, she would swim, or hike out to explore the forest and granite outcroppings every day. She was in college now, but like most of the young folk, she returned to the family home on the river as often as she could.

Jim and Janet, Sanderson were proud to be the second generation living on the Dead River. Jim made a fortune in the stock market which allowed him to retire early. They passed their love of the river on to their four children and, although their children lived out of the area, they came home often with their own children, the third generation to enjoy this pristine wilderness.

Our walk completed, we arrived back at our cottage and I called my friend, John Baldwin to see if he was interested in mountain biking. I didn't have to ask him twice. There were many logging and hiking trails in the area. It was fun to see where a trail led. Occasionally, we had to turn back, but usually it led us on a nice adventure. Often times, it culminated with a beautiful view overlooking the Dead River. It was exhilarating to ride with the wind blowing and the sun shining in my face. Relaxing after our rides, we sometimes revisited memories of a simpler time in our lives:

"Do you remember in fifth grade when Mr. Larson asked you if you had your pocket knife? After you told him you did, he sent you outside to cut some pussy willows for a science project." We both smiled at the idea of taking a pocketknife to school today, and even more humorous was the idea of a teacher sending a student outside during class to cut pussy willows.

"Do you remember Dave Downs?" John asked.

"Yes." I said. "We used to ride the bus together. I heard he lost his wife to cancer last year. I believe he lived in North Carolina, but is planning to move here permanently since she passed."

"Yeah. He was the manager of a chemical plant. He is building a house on the north side of the Dead River now. I saw him last week in Walmart.

"And whatever happened to Susan Maconi?" I asked. "Didn't you get in trouble for kissing her on the junior high basketball bus?"

"Yes, but it was worth it," John replied with a smile.

With our ride completed we returned home to look forward to more excitement on the Dead River.

The next day was the last Saturday in June. Everyone looked forward to the Campers' Group fireworks display on the river. Hundreds of boats filled to capacity assembled in the widest bay in the river, often tying up to one another to enjoy an evening of fun and comradery while waiting for the show to start. Once darkness fell, the pyrotechnic display was spectacular. My favorites were the "Weeping Willow" explosions. Watching the boats parade by, return to their cottages up and down the river with their running lights turned on, was spectacular as well. The partying continued on dry land; silhouettes of campfires shimmered in the river as children ran in and out of the water, way past their bedtimes, or falling asleep in their mother's arms. One by one, the campfires were extinguished as the merry-makers crawled into bed.

The next morning, Barb and I had coffee on the deck, and then were strolling along the beach, when my phone rang. It was John. "It's a perfect day to ride," he said.

When I told my wife who called, she merely responded "Your water bottle is on the kitchen counter. I washed it last night."

"Thanks," I replied.

After checking my bike tires and brakes, I pedaled to John's house. He was already on his bike and ready to go.

"What do you think about doing the Mulligan Plains?" John asked.

"Sounds great," I said. We rode out into the Jack Pine plains. Turning off the main trail, we saw a dark green Jeep parked on the side of the road, and then moments later, we saw a young lady coming towards us wearing a green running suit, and waved as we passed one another. "Could that have been Jenni Durant? I haven't seen her in years. She must be in good shape to be jogging way up here, that must be her Jeep parked a few miles back," I said.

Jenni was an attractive twenty year old, with long brown hair and brown eyes. She was a junior at Michigan State majoring in Sociology. After graduation, she planned to travel the globe, and then settle down to help the less fortunate in the cities. Jenni was currently doing a summer internship in Chicago.

"Yep, I think that was Jenni," John said. "She must have come home for the fireworks."

Back at John's cottage we sat on some old stumps, and we joked about how much easier biking used to be. Age was catching up with us, but it was good to be alive.

Chapter Two

Except for the holidays, Jenni just didn't have time to come north to the Superior Peninsula and she wanted to make the most of every minute of her four-day vacation. Since her parents were still sleeping, she had left a note on the kitchen table telling them that she was heading out to enjoy some of her favorite old trails. She drove toward the Mulligan Plains, parking her Jeep and ran out four miles to the fork in the trail, deciding that was enough, she turned around. Running back to her Jeep, she had seen two bikers and waved to them as they passed, and that was the last the last thing she remembered. After being struck on the head, everything went black.

By the time Jenni had been loaded, unconscious, into the trunk of a car, John and I had reached the overlook at the end of the logging trail. The view was spectacular. The river slowly meandered toward the dam and boats left fluffy white wake trails shimmering behind them on the waterway. We didn't think anything of it when we noticed the dark green Jeep was still parked in its original location.

A few hours later the phone rang. After a brief discussion, Barb said good-by and hung up the phone. "That was Betty Durant. They don't know where Jenni is. Her Jeep is gone and she left a note that she was jogging. Jenni should have been back by now."

I said, "Did you say a Jeep? John and I passed one on County Road 573. It was just off the road on one of the logging trails."

"I'll call and tell her," Barb said.

Later in the day the phone rang and it was Betty.

Barb said, "Hello, Betty! Any luck finding Jenni? Really? She wasn't there? We'll come right now." Barb looked at me: "We have to help look for Jenny, they found her Jeep, but there was no sign of her."

We climbed into my truck and drove out to the logging trails. Others had come with their four wheel ATVs and some arrived on dirt bikes. We searched for several hours, and then decided that it was time to call the sheriff's department. "Hello, Sheriff. This is Bill Bennett," I said. "Jenni Durant is missing just off County Road 573. John and I saw her jogging this morning on one of the logging trails and her Jeep is still here. We've searched for hours, but there is no sign of her."

"We'll be there as soon as we can. I'll contact the State Police and Search and Rescue," he said.

Sheriff Remington showed up about an hour later. The state police brought in their dog. He and his handler followed the trail out, and then back toward the Jeep, never veering from the trail.

While the dog was sniffing the trail, the Mesabi Emergency Rescue Units started arriving. Sheriff Remington turned his IPhone on, bringing up a map of the Dead River onto his screen. Using GPS coordinates, Sheriff Remington told each member of the search party what area to cover. "And I have contacted the Department of Natural Resources. They'll search along the river's edge," he added. Well after midnight, we regrouped at the Jeep. We'd all come up empty. It seems that Jenni had simply disappeared.

As the rescue vehicles were driving away, John Baldwin pulled up with his travel trailer. He started his generator and turned on the outside lights. The Durants could sleep in the trailer, for what remained of the night.

The next morning, we started searching as soon as we could see our hands in front of our faces. As the sun rose higher in the sky, more people came to help. The Emergency Rescue Units returned, using ATVs, so that they could cover a lot more terrain than we could on foot. A helicopter flew overhead and scoured the entire area.

Gathering back together at noon, we compared notes. The Durants were frantic. None of Jenni's friends had heard from her. John and I returned to the last area we saw her, but there wasn't a trace. I sympathized with her parents.

"Jim, we will have to keep looking," I said

"I can't stand it," he replied. "She's our only child. I can't imagine going on without her," he said.

Chapter Three

From the trunk of their car, the kidnappers had thrown Jenni into a root cellar. The root cellar was damp, smelled, and was pitch black. Jenni could hardly breathe. Through a slot in the door, they passed her a sandwich and a cup of water. There was only a pail in the corner for her to use as a toilet. What seemed like hours ago, she had quit screaming and she was tired from crying. She was weak and filthy and her head ached. Every time she woke up, she was still locked in the room. Kidnapped. She had no idea how long she had been held captive. She could hear people walking around upstairs, but when she tried to get their attention, there was no response. In her history class, she had read about the Holocaust survivors. Some of them made it because they had the will to live. She would have that same will.

On the floor above her head, the kidnappers discussed her fate. "Do you think we will get more for her than the others?" Ace Wilson asked.

"We should. But we have to wait until we get in touch with Fernando. She will bring a nice price on the market," Larry Fender replied.

Years before, the two cousins had served time in the La Mesa Prison in Tijuana for human trafficking. After the riots in 2008, they were given early parole to reduce overcrowding. After they were released, they headed north of the border, traveling around the country as day laborers for line drivers. The drivers would pull into a truck stop and ask if anybody wanted to work for cash. They'd work a few days, and then move on to another truck stop until they ran out of money. Eventually, they stole a car and began kidnapping young prostitutes who hung out at the truck stops. They'd sedate the women, drive them across the border and sell them in Mexico. Because prostitutes were pretty invisible, nobody missed them and the customs agents never suspected anything. They enjoyed this lifestyle for several years.

They had ridden with a line driver into Needleton, where they unloaded a shipment. Cash in hand, they walked the streets, ending up in a local bar called *Rocky's*. It was managed by the former owner's wife, Connie Timmerman. Her husband had been killed in a drug deal last winter.

"We're new in town," they told her. "Do you have any suggestions for a cheap place to stay?" Larry Fender asked.

"You looking for work?" Connie asked the two drifters. "I could use a couple of handymen to mop the floors every morning and do other chores. I will pay you five dollars an hour each, plus a place to stay. It's my husband's old house," Connie said.

"We'll take it, but we don't usually stay long in one place," Fender said.

"Throw your gear in the back room; you can get started right now. I'll take you over to the house after work," Connie said.

Later that night, Connie let the drifters into Timmerman's old house. "You can stay here as long as you work for me," she said.

Once Connie had left, Larry Fender and Ace Wilson explored the house. Standing in the old root cellar, it dawned on them that it would be a perfect place to keep the women until they could transport them to Mexico. They reinforced the door, and then cut a slot for passing in food and water.

Fender and Wilson started driving around town in the old car they found in the garage, looking for possible victims. Saturday night they drove to the public boat landing on the Dead River, pretending to watch the fireworks while perusing the parked vehicles. It was mostly friends and families, or young women with boyfriends. The Needleton police sergeant was talking to a gorgeous blond. They sure didn't want any part of him.

The next morning, Larry called out, "Hey, cousin, I've been thinking. Let's take a drive to that boat landing. Maybe, some girls fell asleep on the beach; they might be easy pickings." Larry Fender said.

"That sounds good to me," Ace Wilson replied.

The boat landing was empty, so they drove back through Victorious, then north on County Road 573. They spotted a young woman driving a Jeep. Fender and Wilson looked at each other and smiled. When she parked in the pull-off near the beginning of a logging road, they grinned.

Jenni headed off down the trail. Moments later, two mountain bikers approached and waved as they sped by. They walked down the trail and sat behind a sizeable tree stump. Ace and Fender made themselves as comfortable as they could, sitting on the ground, a small, but a thick and heavy branch at hand. Eventually, they heard the pounding of feet. Waiting until the last minute, Larry bounded out from behind a stump and swung the limb at the back of the runner's head. She went down with a thud. At first, he thought he might have killed her.

The kidnappers duck taped her hands and feet and dropped her in the trunk, slamming it shut.

Fender threw her IPod into the back seat and sped back to Timmerman's house.

"Boy was that easy," Ace bragged.

"Yeah. If they're all that easy, we'll be millionaires in no time," Larry agreed.

Once inside Timmerman's garage, they closed the door, opened the trunk, and carried Jenni down to the root cellar.

Ace said, "Maybe, we could get $50,000 for her."

Larry said, "Yes. All we have to do is keep her alive. She should bring a lot more than the others, considering the shape she is in. I got a map, but it's not very good. We'll have to get a phone with a GPS if we want to find the fastest way to Mexico," Larry said.

"Connie has one… in her purse under the bar," Ace mused.

"And there are some pistols in her office," Larry said.

"And a shotgun in the broom closet," Ace added.

Ace said, "Call Fernando tomorrow, Get straightened out on the price? Tell him we'll have two. If we're going that far, we might as well make it worthwhile."

They looked at each other and smiled.

Chapter Four

Tyler and Officer Dalrymple checked the bars in Needleton to see if anyone had heard anything; I drove my pontoon boat up and down the Dead River looking for clues and Mark and Ben spent time pounding the pavement for clues in the neighboring towns.

The Durants offered a $10,000 reward and put up posters in many Victorious and Needleton businesses. Sunday afternoon, Ken Durant entered *Rocky's*; Ace Wilson and Larry Fender were mopping the floor.

"Is it okay if I put a reward poster with a picture of our daughter in your window?" Ken asked.

"Sure, the owner's in the office, but I don't think she'd mind. Go ahead," Larry replied smiling.

Looking at the poster's picture, Ace said, "She sure is a pretty thing."

Ken Durant said, "Yes, she is. She's our only daughter."

Larry smiled, "Good luck finding her."

Larry took out a wrinkled piece of paper from his pocket, and walked over to the bar's phone. He dialed the phone number, speaking in Spanish.

"What did he say?" Ace asked with hopeful eyes.

"We have a deal," Larry said.

Smirking, Larry took down the reward poster and tore it up. They both laughed.

Their shift ended at 4:00. Connie paid them in cash, turned the *Closed* sign over to *Open,* and turned the lights on behind the bar. Well supplied with beer, they headed out to the boat landing to enjoy the evening on the beach. Inebriated and enjoying the warm temperatures and the sound of the waves, they fell asleep.

My cell phone rang and I knew beforehand who it probably was on the other end. I picked up the cell phone and listened to a familiar voice.

"Hey… about Jenni Durant. I think we should check out the boat landing. Maybe, someone there has seen something," John Baldwin said.

I was ready when John pedaled up. ""Good idea. There'll be a lot of people around the boat launch and beach boating today. We sure turned up nothing yesterday on the trail."

We headed out, taking the Mid-way exit and continuing toward Basin Drive. The state boat landing wasn't too far down.

Kelly Sanderson, a chemical engineer working for DuPont in Mount Clemens, was the youngest of the four Sanderson children and a fourth-level expert in Tai Kwan Do. Home for fireworks and 4th of July holiday week, she had heard about the disappearance of Jenni Durant and had been reluctant to go running on her own. Still, she knew that there would be tons of people at the boat launch and along the beach. Heading toward the boat landing, she could see there were a few trucks, their boat trailers already unloaded. The fishermen were making an early day of it.

As she jogged past the launch site, a vehicle pulled onto the road and steadily gained ground on her. She moved farther over onto the shoulder to give them plenty of space to pass, but the car continued to follow close behind, matching her speed. Suddenly, the car pulled alongside, swerved directly into her, and knocked her down. Larry and Ace jumped out. Wilson grabbed her arms and Fender struck her in the jaw.

"Open the trunk," Larry Fender ordered.

Ace obeyed and Larry dropped her in, slamming the trunk shut.

At that moment, John and I biked around the corner. Seeing the two men standing in the road next to their car, we stopped and I asked, "Is everything okay?"

"Yes, we're just admiring the river," Ace Wilson said.

Larry said, "My cousin is a shutterbug; he's thinking about

doing a series of pictures of life along the river." Just then, we heard screaming and a thud from inside the trunk. Both men jumped into the vehicle, spun around, and sped off. We gave chase, but just couldn't keep up.

"I want to report a 207 in progress. We think that two men have kidnapped another girl. They're driving a white 1996 Oldsmobile." I gave the dispatcher the license plate number, the location of the kidnapping, then added some general descriptions of the men: "Both were Caucasian. One was about thirty years old, with a receding hair line. He was about six foot tall, weighing around one hundred and eighty pounds. He had a dagger tattoo on his right arm. The other one was about twenty five years of age, with long shaggy hair, and a skull and cross bone tattoo on his neck. He was about five foot eight inches tall, weighing about one hundred and fifty pounds."

Sheriff Remington came around the bend with his flashers on and a police team combed the area for clues, but nothing turned up. Worse yet, as quickly as we had acted, the white Oldsmobile seemed to have vanished. Although cops were on the lookout almost immediately, somehow Fender and Wilson had eluded the dragnet. They were already safely tucked into the garage at the Timmerman house on Pine Street. But Kelly wasn't going to be subdued easily – she was still screaming and kicking the back seat out of the Oldsmobile.

Opening the trunk, Fender and Wilson wrestled her to the ground, Ace grabbed an electrical tie and bound her hands. They carried her into the basement, Kelly twisting and turning, fighting them all the way. But they were persistent. They opened the root cellar door and shoved her in. Even with deadly Tai Kwan Do kicks, she was unable to break through the door. Larry and Ace breathed a sigh of relief. They had just doubled their money on the market in Mexico.

"That's one feisty bitch. She's a real wild cat," Larry commented.

Catching his breath, Ace added, "We'll have to watch her close. She is tougher than the other one."

"Yeah. And those two bikers got a pretty good look at us and probably got the license plate number," Fender said.

Wilson added, "We're out of here. Let's get that phone – we'll need the GPS maps and we better switch vehicles, too."

As Kelly's eyes adjusted to the darkness, she could make out the other young woman. "Who are you?" Jenni asked Kelly.

"Kelly Sanderson. Who are you?" Kelly asked.

"I'm Jenni Durant. I'm the one who was kidnapped a couple of days ago." Jenni said. The two women embraced.

"I know." Kelly replied. "Your parents put up reward posters all over the county. With all this going on, I bet my parents have called the cops by now, too. I should have been back at the cottage by now."

Chapter Five

That night, the team — Mark, Ben, John, Tyler, Carolyn, and I — met at *Geno's Pizzeria*. Carolyn Raft had become a regular in our group. Tyler seemed to like that. We were greeted as usual by a smiling Rick Bonnetelli. After ordering beer and pizza, Tyler brought us up to speed regarding the missing Sanderson girl.

John and I would inquire in Needleton, Ben and Mark would go door to door to the Victorious businesses. Tyler and Carolyn would keep their eyes and ears open around the station and in the lab. We knew time was of the essence.

At *Rocky*'s the next morning, Tyler and Officer Dalrymple questioned Connie Timmerman about the where-abouts of the two suspects who seemed have been involved in the Sanderson kidnapping. Hearing the descriptions, she immediately confirmed that they were dead-ringers for Larry Fender and Ace Wilson.

"Do you know where we could find them?" Tyler Baldwin queried.

"Sure. I'm only paying them $5 an hour, but I am letting them stay for free at Tom's old house."

"Did Tom have a car?" Tyler asked.

"Yes, in fact, he did," Connie answered. "His 1996 white Oldsmobile is still in the garage."

The officers drove over to the suspects' residence. Peering into the garage at Timmerman's house, they saw the white Oldsmobile. The license plate matched exactly. Tyler called the dispatcher: "The suspects are at 103 Pine Street."

Entering the garage, they looked through the vehicle's windows. The bloody IPod on the back seat gave them additional probable cause to enter the building. As the door creaked open, Tyler barked: "Needleton Police!"

But there was no answer. Searching room by room, it was clear that from the bread crumbs and a pail of excrement that the girls had been held captive in the root cellar.

Tyler called in the new information: "Suspects are at large. Premises vacated." Wearing latex gloves to retrieve the IPod from the back seat of the Oldsmobile, he slipped it into an evidence bag.

"Maybe, this will help. We might be able to get some fingerprints and I know who to bring it to," Tyler said smiling.

Entering the M.E.'s laboratory, he asked Carolyn if she could have one of the lab rats run a fingerprint check on this IPod. .

"I can check with Don in forensics."

Fifteen minutes later she was back. "Don's on it... he'll check for fingerprints and run them through the computer. No guarantee, but it might turn up something," Carolyn said.

"How about a drink at *Reflections* later tonight?" Tyler asked hopefully.

"That's not much of an offer." Carolyn said coyly.

"I think it's a pretty good deal from where I'm standing," Tyler said,.

"Pick me up at eight and don't be late," Carolyn smiled at her rhyme.

Tyler smiled.

As he entered his cruiser, the dispatcher was reporting that a late model black panel van had been stolen over on Elm Street. Upon questioning him, the owner reported that he had left the key in the car out front while unloading the groceries, then was going to drive the car around back to the garage. When he came out for the last load, the van was gone.

A quick conversation with the neighbor next door revealed that she had seen two men and two young women getting into the van. Since it was parked along the street with its doors open, she figured that they were friends of the family, borrowing the van for personal reasons. Her description of the four people confirmed what they already suspected. Tyler called in the new information.

Larry looked at Ace and said, "We gotta lay low for a day or so … and I know a place that might work. This guy I met the other night at *Rocky'*, he hates the cops as much as we do. He lives on Barnum Street in Victorious."

When they knocked on the door, a voice called out "Who's there?"

"It's Larry and Ace, from *Rocky's* the other night."

Opening the door a crack, Jack Storm looked out at them. He'd had plenty of run-ins with the law and spent plenty of time in the county jail. "What do you want?" he asked.

"We need a place to hide, just for the night, you know. The police are after us. We have two girls we're taking to Mexico," Larry said.

"What's in it for me?" Jack Storm asked.

"We'll cut you in for a third."

"Bring the girls in and put them in the basement; you can park the van out back between the shed and the woodpile."

Larry Fender and Ace Wilson retrieved the girls. Even with their hands tied behind their backs, they didn't go easily. It took all three men to get them onto the landing of the basement stairs and slam the door behind them.

"Not to worry; there are no windows, or doors down there. They can't go anywhere," Storm said.

"One of you can take the couch; the other gets the chair or the floor.

"Fine with us," said Larry, taking the couch.

After Jack Storm had closed his bedroom door, Ace asked, "Why are you promising that guy one third of our money? He sure didn't earn it."

"Don't worry, cousin. We'll get rid of him."

Morning came quick. After a cup of coffee, they opened the basement door and walked down the stairs.

"Come on sweethearts. Let's get moving."

They pushed the girls upstairs.

"We have to use the bathroom," Kelly said.

"Boy, you're high maintenance," Larry replied. "One at a time and don't try any funny stuff. I'll be checking the bathroom after you're through."

When Jenni was done, Kelly took her turn. When they finished, Larry took one quick look into the bathroom, then pushed the girls toward the back door. Ace brought the van as close to the door as he could and Larry shoved them in. Not even bothering to lock up the house, Jack jumped in too. No way was he going to be tricked out of his share.

Larry looked at Jack and said, "We're gonna make a stop before we hit the road. We need a phone and some guns."

"Sounds good," Storm said.

Larry pulled into the alley behind *Rocky's Bar*. "Stay here and keep a sharp eye. And keep those girls quiet," Larry said to Ace and Jack.

He entered through the back door of the bar, and looked around. He saw Connie in the office doing paperwork. Walking quietly across the floor, Larry Fender reached behind the bar and picked up her purse. In the process, a glass crashed to the floor. Connie came out. Larry had opened her bag and was reaching in. "What are you doing? Get out now! The police are looking for you!" Connie screamed.

Larry took the phone and the wallet, picked up the black jack that her husband had kept under the bar and took several steps toward her. She ran into the office, but Larry smashed the door open before she could lock it. Shoving her into the wall, he grabbed the two hand guns from the top drawer of her desk. Pointing one at Connie, he backed out of the office, and then took her former husband's shotgun from the broom closet near the back door on his way out.

As part of their daily rounds, Tyler Baldwin and Officer Dalrymple had been looping past the bar regularly since Ace and Larry had disappeared. They were passing by just as Larry Fender was walking toward the van. Jumping out of the cruiser, Glocks raised, they shouted, "You! In the vehicle! Keep your hands on the dashboard. Nobody move." Jack Storm charged out of the van, toward Tyler. Tyler fired once. Storm staggered, and then fell face down. Tyler ordered Larry to lie down. Instead, Larry raised the shot gun and fired. Tyler dived to the ground, but not before he was hit. Larry fired again and Officer Dalrymple fell against the cruiser, and then slumped to the ground. Larry jumped in behind the wheel of the van and sped off.

Tyler could barely talk. "444" he gasped into the radio. "Repeat 444." He fell unconscious.

Police cruisers arrived, followed by EMTs who worked frantically on both Tyler and Officer Dalrymple. Carolyn pulled into to the alley, running to Tyler. Sheriff Remington had called her, thinking she would want to be there. She could tell he was in critical condition.

Looking over to her left, she saw the EMTs shake their heads, then cover Officer Dalrymple's with a sheet as several officers knelt down by the body, closing their eyes. He left behind a young widow and two children.

Carolyn turned back to Tyler and asked the EMT in charge, "What do you think? Tell me the truth."

"He's been shot in the stomach and right arm. He has multiple wounds. We are trying to stop the bleeding. I'm afraid he may bleed out before we get him to the emergency room," the senior EMT reported.

They raised the gurney, carefully sliding him into the ambulance.

"Can I ride with him?" Carolyn asked.

"Get in," the senior EMT said, securing Tyler to the bed. Carolyn held his hand as they sped toward the Victorious Hospital.

Chapter Six

When they heard the news, Tyler's parents John and Valerie rushed to the hospital. They were met by Carolyn in the surgery waiting room. Mark, Ben and I rushed in moments later.

"How is he?" John asked.

"No prognosis yet," Carolyn Raft replied.

Valerie began to sob. John showing emotion for one of only a few times, put his arm around his wife.

"He'll pull through. He's tough," John said trying to sound reassuring.

Sheriff Remington entered the room right behind us.

"How is he doing?" Sheriff Remington asked.

John repeated his answer. We sat quietly for several hours while Tyler fought for his life. The strain on everyone's face was apparent. It's amazing how time stands still in a crisis.

Sheriff Remington leaned over to Mark, Ben and me and said, "Jack Storm is dead. They must have holed up at his house last night. Also, we searched the Timmerman residence and found a rough map of their escape route. They're headed to Monterrey, Mexico. We're guessing he's with his cousin, Ace Wilson. The two of them have done hard time in a Mexican prison for human trafficking and it sounds like they're at it again. By the way, the fingerprints came back on Jenni's IPod. They belong to Larry Fender. No surprise there."

Doctor Bell emerged from the emergency operating area. "We don't know if he is going to pull through. Some of the fragments ruptured his kidney. He has lost a lot of blood, and he may lose his right arm. There was severe damage to the artery above the elbow. Right now we have to wait. If he can make it through the night, he might have a chance."

"Can we see him?" Valerie asked.

"He is sedated, but you can see him. He won't know you are there," Dr. Bell responded then led them through the double doors.

We sat with Carolyn and prayed. We had been through this many times. It was in God's hands now. When John and Valerie Baldwin returned, they were both white as ghosts. "He's as good as can be expected, but we won't know until morning," Valerie said. We braced for a long night as we settled in.

The next morning, Doctor Bell reported that they'd successfully stopped the bleeding and that Tyler was holding his own. It was the glimmer of hope that we all had been praying for. We embraced, and made our way out of the waiting room.

"Let's get these bastards," I said, "even if we have to track them to the end of the Earth." Mark and Ben nodded.

Chapter Seven

After packing a few changes of clothes and all the weapons we could carry, we rendezvoused at the Mesabi County Courthouse. Sheriff Remington was there to see us off. "I can't condone what you are going to do, but good luck. I'll do what I can to help you," he said, handing us a photocopy of the map from Timmerman's house with a sly smile. "I'll keep you posted; you do the same. And I'll call ahead and alert all the police along the route. Good luck!"

We knew they had a head start, but we had to catch them. Mark had his Super Sport Camaro. It could flat out fly. We threw as much as we could into the trunk, and then put the rest of our clothes and weapons in the back seat. It didn't leave much room, but we'd sacrifice comfort for speed.

Ben set up his Motorola LTI portable encrypted police scanner — it could operate from any place that Wi-Fi could pick up a signal — and we were off for Detroit. From there, they'd planned to go through Gary, Indiana, then Springfield, Missouri, and on to Oklahoma City, Fort Worth and then to Laredo. That is, if they hadn't plotted a new route, perhaps through Chicago. We knew we had to intercept them before they reached Mexico, or we'd never catch them.

As we got closer to Detroit, Sheriff Remington called. "Good news" he said. Tyler is still holding his own. And the Detroit Metro Police have spotted a black van with matching plates at the Red Roof Inn off I-75. They're closing in." I looked at the GPS. We weren't that far away. Mark accelerated.

We approached the Red Roof Inn. We could see lights flashing. "Any luck?" I asked the nearest officer.

"Nope, they slipped away. You must be the guys from the

Superior Peninsula," he replied.

I said, "Yes, we're on their trail, we're trying to save the two kidnapped girls."

Ben Myers took a turn behind the wheel and continued west toward Gary, Indiana stopping only for gas, fast food and restroom breaks. My phone sounded about 3:00 a.m. "A fast food restaurant employee confirmed a black van with the two men fitting their descriptions drove through about one hour ago in Gary," Sherriff Remington announced. "The employee remembers there were four people: two white males in the front and two young females in the back seat. It was the girls' pleading looks and filthy running clothes that caught his attention."

At least we knew we were on the right track. We had feared that they were taking a different route all together, or maybe sticking to the back roads. We figured that they must feel pretty confident. Not overly confident, though, or maybe they were just smart… because minutes later, Ben's portable scanner picked up some Chicago PD chatter. The Illinois state police had found an abandoned black van at Chicago O'Hare International Airport Terminal. If they had stolen a car from one of the airport parking lots, we might not know it for weeks.

The break we needed came unexpectedly. At 7:00 a.m. while we were refueling at one of the toll road plazas, Ben heard more chatter on the scanner. The Chicago Police Department reported that a GMC Suburban had been stolen from a Hertz Rent-a-Car drop-off area. I wrote down the license number and we swung onto the exit ramp leading toward Springfield, Missouri.

At 3:00 p.m., my phone rang again.

"Tyler is coming around." John announced. "He was able to talk a little bit today. He has feeling in his right arm and his blood pressure is stable. They don't know about internal damage, but things are looking up. How's it going on your end?" John asked.

"Thanks for the great news! We're doing all right, cruising on I-64 toward Springfield, Missouri, taking turns driving. Mark's snoring drives us crazy, but we're making good time. Sheriff Remington is keeping us posted; we also learned that the kidnappers switched vehicles in Chicago. Say "hello" to your family for us, and tell the Durants and Sandersons that we're doing our best to find their girls," I said.

Driving through Springfield, Missouri with Mark at the wheel, the chatter on the scanner reported that a dark Suburban had been spotted at a BP gas station in a southwest suburb called Elwood. Checking the GPS, we realized that we were only a few miles away. We turned off I-44 and pulled into the station.

The Suburban was parked at the pumps, with the engine running. A Missouri state trooper was parked behind the station waiting for back up. We were the back up.

Mark steered right toward the Suburban, blocking its escape. When Ace Wilson sauntered out of the station, he quickly realized that the escape route was blocked, which meant that someone was onto them. He pulled out his pistol and fired at us. The bullets penetrated our windshield. Mark shrieked in pain. Ben and I slid out the passenger side door and scurried around behind the car.

The Missouri State Trooper pulled alongside our vehicle, slid out of his cruiser and fired at Ace Wilson. Wilson staggered to the Suburban. Larry Fender pulled him in, and threw it into reverse, smashing into the vehicle behind him. Wilson continued to fire as they drove away, shooting out our front tire and sending the Missouri State Trooper down on one knee in pain.

The fugitives disappeared into the sea of speeding traffic on the interstate. Other police officers arriving quickly on the scene aimed their pistols at us and ordered us to put our hands up. We did as we were told. EMTs arrived, tending to both Mark and the wounded trooper. We explained who we were. Checking with their dispatcher, they were informed that we were legitimate, but that the criminals, still holding their hostages, had gotten away.

Several hours later in the surgical waiting room at Ozarks Community Hospital, Ben reported that Mark had come through surgery just fine, but that the state trooper was touch and go. "Your friend's prognosis is good," the surgeon reported. "Your friend was wounded in the shoulder. It's not life threatening, but he has to remain in the hospital for several days.

"I can stay with him," Ben offered. I nodded, then shook Ben's hand. "No time to waist," I said.

"Good luck!" he replied.

Getting back to the BP and changing the tire was a piece of cake. As I got back on the road, I headed toward Oklahoma City. The sun was setting as I spotted the city lights in the distance. I kept my eyes open for the exit lane: From Oklahoma City, I had to take I-35 to Fort Worth, Texas. Moments later, my phone rang.

"How are you doing?" Sheriff Remington asked.

"We made contact at a gas station in Springfield, Missouri, but they got away. Mark was wounded and had to have surgery to repair his shoulder. Ben's staying with him. Ace was also wounded. He is going to need medical attention. Can you alert the local police to contact trauma centers between here and Fort Worth? I'm headed that way, but I am going to have to pull over soon and get some sleep. How is Tyler doing?"

"Tyler had to go back into surgery. He was running a fever, which means some kind of infection," Sheriff Remington said.

Chapter Eight

Ace dived toward the Suburban and Larry pulled him the rest of the way in. As they sped away, Ace kept shooting back toward the trooper and the other car. Once on the highway, both cousins realized the extent of Ace's injury.

"A doctor. I gotta see a doctor," Wilson said.

"We can't stop now. We'll have to wait. If we pull over, we'll be arrested for sure," Larry Fender warned.

The two girls, who were bound and gagged, started squirming in the back seats, taking advantage of the confusion to try to get out.

"Sit still, or I'll just shoot the both of you right now." Kelly glared at her kidnappers. When she got the chance, she would kill them. Jenni started crying.

"What are you looking at? Once we get you to Mexico, you're going to wish you were never born," Fender barked as he scowled at Kelly. Then he looked at Wilson. "Don't worry, Ace; we'll get you taken care of," he said.

As they approached Carthage, Missouri, he could see the Mercy Hospital sign in the distance. He pulled into the parking lot.

"I'll be right back," Larry told Ace.

Larry stepped out of the vehicle, and then walked across the parking lot and into the emergency room. There were five people in line at the admission desk and the clerk was busily asking questions and entering the responses into the electronic medical records system. When someone walked out through the double doors, Fender slipped through the door. Inside, it was organized chaos. Every room seemed to be occupied. Following a nurse into the room marked *Dispensary*, he grabbed her from behind and put his knife to her throat, asking, "Do you want to live?"

When she nodded, he pulled the knife away. He turned her around asking, "What's your name?"

"Shirley," she blurted out.

"Well Shirley, we're going to take a little walk. I have a friend in the parking lot. He's been shot and you're coming out to help me. Take whatever medical supplies you'll need."

Gathering up antibiotic cream, gauze, scissors and tape, they walked side-by-side out of the emergency room. No one even looked up. Shirley prayed that someone would see them, or that the security camera would pick them up on the video and send help.

When Larry opened the Suburban's front passenger car door, Ace almost fell out. Shirley took one look and said, "He is going into shock. He has to see a doctor. Let me take him into the ER."

Larry Fender said, "No way. You treat him right here."

When she unbuttoned his shirt, blood flowed freely. Shirley said, "I can hear a sucking sound. His chest cavity has been punctured and he is coughing up blood. He needs emergency surgery. Now."

Larry replied, "Just patch him up."

"You," she said to Larry, "I need you to apply pressure on the wound." To Wilson, she said, "Hold your breath while I wrap the bandage around you." She wound it around several times until it was snug. "This isn't going to help very much; if you want to live, you must be seen right away,"

"That'll have to do," said Fender. He turned quickly, striking the nurse on the back of the head with the butt of his pistol. She fell to the ground. Fender shut the passenger door, walked around the Suburban, and got behind the wheel, then drove, away into the night.

As they made their way toward the interstate, Fender realized his cousin probably wasn't going to survive. He wasn't sure he'd even miss him. He could do the negotiating with Fernando himself once he got the two girls to Monterrey.

He slowed down. With no cars coming in either direction, he

reached over, opened the passenger door, lifted up his right leg, and with a quick motion, kicked Wilson out of the Suburban onto the side of the road. Reaching over, he pulled the door shut, and then increased his speed. There wasn't a soul in sight. The two girls sat looking out the back window, horrified.

Chapter Nine

I called Ben to see how Mark was recovering. "How is the patient?" I asked,.

"He is a little ornery, but with him it's hard to tell," Ben responded.

"What's his prognosis?" I asked.

"He is a royal pain in the behind," Ben said laughing.

I could hear Mark telling him to shut up.

"Where are you?" Ben shouted into the phone.

"I'm approaching Fort Worth on I- 35," I replied.

"Well, good luck. I'm putting up with this old coot. I should have gone after them, and you should have stayed here," Ben said.

I smiled as I ended the call, but quickly realized that I just couldn't drive anymore. I pulled over into a state rest area, closed my eyes and instantly fell asleep.

Back in Mesabi County, the Durants and Sandersons wanted all the details, both on what Sheriff Remington was doing and how our pursuit was going. He assured them that every law enforcement officer between here and Laredo had been notified and that the FBI had been called in to assist with the case. Even with hourly updates, the mothers were hysterical.

After the latest update, Janet Sanderson sobbed "Wh... what are we going to do?"

"We are going to be resourceful," her husband replied, and then he took out his IPhone, and called his neighbor on the Dead River, Loren Luft.

"Hello," said Loren.

"Hello, Loren, this is Jim Sanderson. I will get right to the point. You know our daughter and Jenni Durant are missing.

We think they have been kidnapped. Who was that big guy you called last year when you needed help?"

There was a long pause on the other end.

Loren Luft replied, "His name was John Crane and he was as smart and tough as they come, but he's dead. His body was found in the river. I can give you his cell number, though. Maybe, he had a partner."

After thanking Loren for the information, Jim dialed the number Loren had given him. Nobody answered, but Jim left a voice message describing the situation in detail along with his IPhone number. He prayed he was doing the right thing.

An hour later, his cell phone rang.

Jim answered the phone: "Hello, this is Jim Sanderson."

"Yes, I can pay that. I'll deposit the hundred thousand into your Cayman Island account by the close of business today."

"Yes, I have the account number, and I'll be happy to meet you at the private air terminal."

"One more question… I know that you helped Loren Luft last year. Why does he think you're dead?"

The line went dead before the last question was answered.

The next morning, Jim was waiting at the private air terminal at the Mesabi Airport. A huge man approached him, asking "Are you Sanderson?" Jim Sanderson nodded.

Man-Mountain said, "Don't say a word." Crane nodded toward the parking lot.

"You look good for a dead man," Sanderson said.

John Crane said, "Don't worry about my premature death. Where are the kidnappers taking the girls?"

"From what we can piece together," Jim Sanderson answered, "Ace Wilson and Larry Fender are taking my daughter and another girl named Jenni Durant to Laredo, Texas, then on to Monterrey, Mexico, where they plan to sell the girls into slavery." Jim could barely get the words out.

"I've heard of this before" John Crane continued. "From there they will be transported to Tijuana where they will be filled with methamphetamines and forced into prostitution.

Sanderson shook his head in anguish. He just didn't want to hear anymore.

"If I rescue them, you owe me the second hundred thousand. Don't contact me and don't ask any questions. Understand?" Crane stated.

"Yes,'" Jim Sanderson replied. "You do need to know, though, that some retired law enforcement officers are pursuing them, too. One of them was wounded in Springfield, Missouri and the second stayed behind to care for him. Bill Bennett's the only one still on the trail. You remember him?"

Crane stated, "Yes. He's not too sharp, but a good man. Thanks for the tip. I will keep an eye out for him."

John Crane stood up and headed back to his plane without saying a word

Chapter Ten

As Fender and his victims were driving toward Laredo, Jenni started kicking the driver's seat. That was her way of telling Fender one of them had to relieve themselves.

"Can't you hold it?" Fender asked.

She continued to kick the seat until he pulled over. He opened his door, looking up and down the highway. When no cars were coming, he opened her door, allowing her to step out. He escorted her into the desert, untied her hands, and told her to hurry up.

"Can't you turn around?" Jenni asked.

"Hurry up, or I'll drag you back to the Suburban," he ordered.

He re-tied her hands again and dragged her back to the car, holding her behind the car while another vehicle passed. Taking her by the arm, he walked her around the car to her door. Once the door opened, Fender was struck in the face with the tire iron. As he fell down, Kelly jumped out. Her hands were still tied, but she had managed to retrieve the tire iron from the back. With their captor flat on the roadbed with blood running down his face, Kelly flew out of the Suburban, grabbing Jenni and running toward freedom.

Fender staggered back to the driver's seat, started the car, spun the Suburban around, and drove after them. A minivan approached from the opposite direction.

Seeing the girls' frantic motions, a man and a woman had pulled over to the shoulder and were listening intently to the girls' story.

Fender pulled up, brandishing his pistol.

Fender barked, "Get over here now, or I'll shoot all four of you."

As the girls headed toward the Suburban, Larry Fender shot out the minivan's front and back tires, told the couple to throw their cell phones onto the highway, and shot the cell phones into pieces. Getting slowly out of the vehicle, he approached Kelly, smashed her in the face with his pistol and dragged her into the car. Jenni meekly followed.

"I'm going to kill you," Kelly said.

As they drove away, Fender threatened: "If you do that again, I'll kill you and leave you to rot in the desert."

He drove on, his head throbbing in pain for hours. Seeing a convenience store ahead and needing gas anyway, he pulled into the store, gagged the girls again and stepped out. At the pump, he used Connie's stolen credit card, then drove around to the back of the convenience store and parked.

Fender looked at the girls: "If you want to live, keep quiet. Maybe I'll even bring you some food." He picked up several packs of gauze and bandages, a six pack of beer, and some chips.

"Are you okay, sir?" the young check-out clerk inquired.

"Just tell me how much I owe you," Fender sneered.

The boy said, "That will be $29.85."

Fender swiped Connie Timmerman's stolen credit card, picked up his purchases and walked out, watching a Texas Ranger's flashing lights speed off in the direction he had just come. Someone with a cell phone must have stopped to help the couple in the minivan. Once back in the Suburban, he gradually pulled away, so as not to attract attention. The road sign up ahead announced "Laredo 424." His journey was almost over.

Chapter Eleven

I had been driving all day. I was getting tired, but I had to be closing in. Suddenly, I noticed some people were gathering on the side of the road. They were standing around what looked like a man lying on the ground. I parked my car and walked toward the crowd. Working my way through the curious onlookers, I recognized Ace Wilson. "Water, I need some water," Wilson begged. A Good Samaritan was leaning down to help him.

I shouted, "Don't help him. He's a wanted criminal. He and his cousin kidnapped two young women from Michigan and are planning to sell them in Mexico. I will deal with him." The crowd stepped back. I wanted to choke Wilson.

I looked at Wilson and asked, "Where are the girls?"

Wilson said, "I need some water."

I repeated my question, "Where are the two girls?"

Needing him to stay alive at least for a few more minutes, someone passed me a bottle of water. After he took a gulp, I pulled it away. He opened his eyes and asked, "Who are you?"

I said, "I'm the guy who's going to determine if you live or die."

Ace Wilson pleaded, "I need more water."

I said emphatically "Let me be clear, I don't care if you make it, or not. Tell me where the girls are. I chased you half-way across the country."

Ace Wilson said, "Larry's up ahead about an hour in front of you. He's going to stop at his sister's house in Fort Worth. More water!"

"What's the address?" I asked holding the water in front of him.

Ace Wilson said, "214 Ballinger Street."

I handed him the water. Someone called 911. It wasn't long before a Texas Ranger pulled up and sized up the situation.

I said, "This man and his partner kidnapped two girls from Michigan. I am trying to rescue the girls before they are sold into prostitution in Mexico. His partner must have left him to die rather than stop to seek medical attention."

Once the Ranger had verified my story with his dispatcher, I left Ace in the Ranger's care until the ambulance could arrive, or until he died on the roadside from his wounds. At least I had the information that I needed. I entered the address into my GPS and headed toward Fort Worth.

As I was driving, my phone rang.

"How are you doing?" Sheriff Remington asked.

"Well enough. I just found Ace Wilson lying in a ditch on I-35 – Larry must have kicked him out of the Suburban to die on his own. Ace gave me the information I need. Fender is staying the night at his sister's in Fort Worth ... 214 Ballinger Street."

"Good news. I also wanted you to know that the Sandersons have hired a private detective... an old friend of yours. John Crane is back from the dead. That body we recovered last year from the Dead River couldn't have been Crane's. It must have been someone else's... maybe that escaped convict from Mesabi State Prison we never captured. I suppose Crane killed him and then switched clothes," Sheriff Remington mused.

As I disconnected my cell phone, I had mixed feelings. Crane was the size of a mountain and a very good detective, who had access to amazing resources, but he had punched my lights out last year, and he only worked alone. I guess it would work out if he agreed to cooperate.

After hanging up, Sheriff Remington called Jim Sanderson. "Bill Bennett's in Texas. He just found Ace Wilson barely alive on the side of the road; it seems his cousin kicked him out of the vehicle instead of stopping for medical help. Ace told Bennett where to find Fender in Fort Worth... 214 Ballinger Street. Pass that on to your guy."

When Jim Sanderson called, Man-Mountain picked up his

phone and said, "I thought I told you never to call me."

"I have news. Wilson has been picked up by the Texas Rangers and Bennett is on his way to Fort Worth. Fender is staying at his sister's house... 214 Ballinger Street." Before Sanderson could say good-bye, the line went dead.

John Crane shut off his phone off and directed his pilot to change the flight plan to Fort Worth, not Laredo. The pilot nodded and radioed it in.

Shortly after landing, Crane walked to a rental agency desk. Moments later, he was throwing his gear in the back of a black Humvee. At the first stop light, he typed the address into the GPS and headed into town.

Fender's sister's residence, 214 Ballinger Street, was a rundown two-story house in what looked like an unstable, dangerous, neighborhood. Pulling up to the residence I noticed a few lights were on inside and the black Suburban was parked behind the house. Dusk was settling in. I walked behind the garage and looked into the Suburban. No sign of the girls. Creeping up to one of the back windows, I didn't see Larry Fender's brother-in-law, Clyde Helmon, get up from the kitchen table and walk into another room. The TV flickered on. Fender remained seated at the kitchen table, drinking whiskey in the company of a young woman. They appeared to be arguing.

I leaned closer to the window.

"Why did you come here?" the woman asked. "You know I don't need this. Clyde just got out of prison. He can't be seen with you. He's on parole. You always come back to me when you're in trouble,"

"Listen Clare, you're my sister," Fender replied. "Who else can I turn to? It'll only be for the night. I'll take the girls and leave before sunrise. I just need a place to crash for a few hours. I haven't slept in days."

"Where's cousin Ace?" Clare asked. "He's not dead, is he?"

"He had to leave suddenly," Larry responded.

"They need to eat?" Clare asked, looking toward the girls who were tied up on the floor.

Larry Fender said, "No, I just gave them food."

Clare said, "I don't want them dying like the one last year. I still worry about her being buried in the back yard."

"I'll make it worth your while after I get paid," Fender said.

Clare said, "And you better pay me. I had to bury that girl last year. You still owe me for that. I figured it's worth about ten grand for that job. Plus if you want me to help you get these bimbos across the Rio Grande, I figure they're both worth five thousand each. Now, that brings the total to twenty thousand dollars."

"Listen, Sis, I'll square up as soon as I can sell these two. Fernando promised me fifty thousand a piece. You and Clyde can do a lot with twenty thousand dollars." Clare seemed to agree.

I decided that I couldn't wait for the Fort Worth police. I was going in. I took out my Glock, slowly moved toward the back door, and entered.

I ordered, "Get your hands up."

Both Clare and Fender raised their hands.

Keeping my gun trained on the criminals, I asked the girls if they were OK. They simply nodded.

"They're just fine," Larry Fender said.

Suddenly the girls' eyes widened. I certainly didn't see it coming. Fender's brother-in-law, Clyde, hit me from behind with a lamp and I fell dazed onto the floor. Fender grabbed my Glock, hitting me across the face. The next thing I knew I was being nudged in the stomach. I tried to open my eyes, but I couldn't. "Get up, Stupid."

I immediately recognized the voice: John Crane.

"You sure screwed this up," he continued, disgusted. "They're long gone now. Fender must have taken his sister, her husband and the two girls with him."

"How did I know there was someone hiding in the other room? Besides I thought you were dead."

"Do I look like I'm dead?" John Crane asked. "You should have walked around the exterior of the house, looking in every window." John Crane asked.

"I did, but I didn't know about the brother-in-law. I guess I thought I could take them and stop the madness." Deep down, I knew Crane was right. I should have waited. I just didn't want to admit it.

I asked, "How did you find me?"

"The Sandersons gave me the address you passed on to the Mesabi sheriff," John replied. That was good enough for me. I followed him out of the house.

He looked at me and shook his head. "I don't know if I should send you home, or take you with me. If I send you home I know you'll just try to follow me anyway and screw it up again," I had learned not to disagree with him. "So just leave your car here and come with me. But if you get in my way, I'll dump you."

I nodded, then retrieved a few things from my car including Ben's police scanner. I got into the front seat of his Humvee. I could hear him growl as we drove back onto I-35.

Chapter Twelve

Valerie and John entered the hospital room, looking at their son. Carolyn Raft was holding Tyler's hand. He was still unconscious.

"How is he doing?" they asked.

"He seems to be getting some color back. Doctor Bell was here about an hour ago. He said he is doing as well as can be expected," said Carolyn stroking his hair.

"Thanks for staying with him. He thinks a lot of you," John said.

"I know. I just have such bad history with men. My first husband abused me and I am afraid to commit to someone again. I should have left him sooner, but I was raised with the belief that marriage was forever. Tyler has been nothing, but kind to me. I keep pushing him away because I just don't want to be hurt again."

"I can promise you he will never hurt you," Valerie said.

"That's right," Tyler said weakly.

Carolyn and Valerie both hugged him, starting to cry. Tyler was smiling from ear to ear. It was a Hallmark moment.

Mark had been released from the hospital and Ben picked him up in the rental car. They were barely on their way before they made one wrong turn after another, arguing their way down the interstate toward Fort Worth.

"Hey, Bill! This is Ben. Where are you? What's going on?"

"I have some good news and some bad news," I replied. "The good news is I caught Fender and the two girls. The bad news is that they got away. Fender's brother-in-law bashed me in the head and knocked me out" I said trying not to be ashamed.

"You needed us," Ben said.

"Another surprise. John Crane is back from the dead. The Sandersons are paying him to get their daughter back. We've hooked up. Our last chance is Laredo. It's about one hundred miles from here," I said.

"Laredo's a rough town. Keep your guard up. It's probably good you have Crane. He's not as good as me, but he'll do. We're trying to catch up, but we're still way behind."

As we got closer to Laredo, I turned on the police scanner. We might get lucky and hear something. Leaving the interstate, Crane dialed a speed dial number, talked to someone in a whisper, then hung up. I knew enough not to ask. His phone rang a few minutes later.

"I got it, thanks. I owe you one," John Crane said as he disconnected.

"Fender has a cousin who lives at 218 Chacon Street," he told me. I entered the address into our GPS.

It was a dilapidated building. Crane stared through his night vison goggles for hours. I sat motionless.

Eventually, Crane said, "You stay here. I'm going to get a better look." He crouched down, making his way to a tree in the boulevard in front of the house. I was surprised how fast he climbed the tree. Hours passed, but there was no movement inside. And I had learned my lesson. I stayed put. All of a sudden, there was a tap on my window. It was John Crane. I just about went through the roof – I had no idea how he got down from the tree and came back across the street without me seeing him.

"What's the matter with you?" Crane asked.

"I always look like this when someone scares the hell out of me," I said.

He didn't appreciate the humor.

"There are gang bangers inside smoking grass. I didn't see Fender. We'll have to wait. I doubt if anything is going to happen before daylight," the Man-Mountain said.

He sat back in his seat and closed his eyes. We waited into the early morning hours.

The next thing I remember, I felt a nudge against my side. Opening my eyes, John Crane was offering me something. "I hope you like your coffee black," he said flatly. He was holding two cups of coffee "There's a *Mister Donuts* down the street."

"Thanks, John," I replied. "You bring me to all the fancy places!"

"Shut up," he answered.

I obeyed. I wanted to ask what his plan was, but I knew he would not give me a coherent answer.

My IPhone rang. It was Ben and Mark. They had driven all night and just arrived in Laredo. We met them at *Mister Donuts.* When we pulled up, Ben was scratching his stomach and Mark stepped out gingerly, barely moving from his shoulder surgery. John Crane looked at me and asked, "Is that our back up?"

"They don't look like much, but that's all we have," I answered.

John Crane shook his head, muttering something under his breath.

While John was on his phone, I heard some chatter referring to a shooting and a drug bust at 218 Chacon Street on the portable police scanner. I motioned for John to come over.

"I just heard there was a shooting and a drug bust at Fender's cousin's address. Should we check it out?"

"We might as well. It's the only lead we have," he replied.

We left the rental car in the Mister Donuts' parking lot and all four of us headed out in the Humvee. When we pulled up at the Chacon Street address, several young men were being led away in hand-cuffs and an ambulance was just leaving. My curiosity got the better of me. I strolled over to a Laredo police officer who was working crowd control.

I asked, "What happened?"

"There was a shooting and a drug bust last night. Some guy brought two girls in there; the gang wanted to rape them. He shot one man and then left with the girls." I nodded like I barely cared. I walked back to the Humvee and shared what I had learned.

"I think we can assume it was Larry Fender."

"Indirectly, that might help us. He won't try to get across the border if there's a description of him posted with the border guards. He will probably try to stay out of sight until this blows over," I pointed out. Everyone agreed, but no one had a clue about where he could be hiding.

"Let me make a call," Crane said.

Chapter Thirteen

Larry Fender was scared. He had to get out of Laredo as fast as possible. He'd just had to shoot his way out of a drug house. He couldn't even trust his own cousin. Driving out toward Lake Casa Blanca looking for a place to hide, Fender noticed a young female walking along the side of U.S -59. Clare said, "Don't even think about it. We have enough problems already."

"Be quiet," Fender snarled. "I'm just going to be neighborly." Jenni and Kelly started squirming in the back seat. Clyde hit them both across their faces to quiet them.

Jenni moaned and looked at Clyde. Through the duct tape over her mouth, she said "Water."

He removed the duct tape and handed her a bottle of warm, stale water.

Just then, Larry pulled over toward the girl who was standing by the side of the road. He lowered the passenger window: "What seems to be the problem?" he asked.

"My rental broke down. I am on my way to Laredo International Airport. Can you give me a ride?" the young girl asked.

"Sure, we would be glad to. Hop in. We have plenty of room," said Fender.

Throwing the water bottle to the floor, Jenni yelled: "No! Run for your life!"

The girl dropped her suitcase and ran. Fender jumped out of the vehicle and went off in pursuit, but didn't get far before changing his mind. Several cars were approaching and an abduction in plain sight with witnesses wouldn't look good. Clyde re-taped Jenni's mouth. Fender glared at her and said, "Wait until tonight. You are going to pay big time."

He accelerated, disappearing down U.S.-59, passing the exit

for the Laredo International Airport, and continued toward Lake Casa Blanca. Fender regretted he didn't have another hostage to sell.

Chapter Fourteen

Fender pulled up to a run-down ranch house. He stepped out of the vehicle, knocked on the front door and waited for an answer. "Just a minute, I'm coming," said the older lady. She opened the door. "What do you want? You must be in trouble, or you wouldn't be here," Mother Fender said.

"Is that anyway to greet your children? Larry Fender asked.

"What is it?" Mother Fender asked.

"We had a little trouble and need a place to stay for a few days," Clare said.

"That's what I thought," the mother said, "The only time I see you is when you need me."

"Could we park our Suburban in the barn?" Fender asked.

Mother Fender said, "I suppose I can't say no."

Larry maneuvered the Suburban over to the barn, opened the door and drove the vehicle inside. After closing the big barn door, he opened the back door of the vehicle and dragged the two girls out. He tied them to a beam, telling them to lie down. They did as they were told, but Fender hit them until they stopped moving. They knew that soon they were going to wish they were dead.

"I'll see you later tonight," he threatened.

Larry returned to the main house. He'd hole up here for a few days. Casa Blanca wasn't far from the Rio Grande. He could slip across at night with the girls to Nuevo Laredo. His sister, Clare and her husband Clyde could go back home once he was across. Fender only had to pacify his mother for a few days. God, he despised her.

Watching the evening news, they saw the police surround and force their way into Cousin Fernando's house. He realized he'd been tricked... Fernando wanted to add them to his own stable of little whores right there in Laredo. There would be no fifty thousand dollars for each of the girls. Fernando's help smuggling the girls over to Monterrey was off. Fender would have to get them across the border and sell them himself. He could surely make it work.

John Crane hung up the phone. "Larry Fender's mom lives on the outskirts of Laredo. She lives off the grid. No telephone; no driver's license; no taxes."

Crane sure had connections that I couldn't imagine. "How in the world did you locate her?" I asked.

"She had a hysterectomy twenty years ago at the Laredo Medical Center," Crane replied,

I said in disbelief, "But those records had to have been discarded years ago."

"Let's just say that there is a higher government that oversees yours," Crane said.

Nodding, but for once not wanting to know more, I said, "That works for me."

We got into the car, heading for Mother Fender's house. We were within a few miles of the ranch when John Crane stopped the car.

"We'll park here and go the rest of the way on foot." By now, we knew better than to ask questions. I told Mark to stay with the car; he looked pretty weak. He didn't argue.

John took a Glock out of his bag, throwing it to me. "Try not to lose that one," he said smugly. Ben, Crane and I headed out across two miles of hot, bleak land. When we got within a quarter mile of the house, John said, "Now we inch the rest of the way." I did not have an affinity for rattlesnakes, or scorpions, but we had no choice. We got on our bellies and crawled.

It took us over an hour to complete the last 450 yards.

About a hundred yards from the house, John took out his binoculars. After a long pause, he turned and said, "I think Fender is in there and he has company. We'll wait for nightfall."

Just before the sun set, the front door opened. Larry Fender walked across the yard toward the barn. Ben and I started to rise up, but John quickly motioned for us to stop.

"No. There's nothing we can do now. We wait until it's dark." It was hard to remain motionless hearing the noise coming from the barn. I closed my eyes, trying to think of something else. After a while, we watched as the lights in the house went on, then hours later, as the lights started to go off. John turned to us: "It's time. I doubt if they have a basement. Ben, you go around back. Bill, you charge the front door. You two take care of whoever is inside. I'll get Fender in the barn. It all goes down in thirty minutes. We synchronized our watches. Ben had the farthest to go, so he set out first, creeping around the car and making his way toward the ranch. I inched my way forward. John departed in the other directions, toward the barn.

At the designated time, Ben crashed through the back door, with Glock in hand. I smashed in the front door and cornered Clyde Helmon, who was sleeping on the couch. "Don't even think about it." I said as Clyde reached for the pistol. Mother Fender and Clare Helmon came running out of their bedroom. Ben aimed his Glock at Fender's sister and mother. They stopped, putting their hands in the air.

"Face down on the floor," I ordered. Still covering the women, I walked over and picked up Clyde's pistol. I pulled out a wrist tie, binding his hands behind his back, and then secured his legs. Ben handled Clare and I took care of their mother.

"Fender's in the barn?" I asked.

They nodded.

We heard a crash and Ben and I looked at each other, smiling. We opened the front door, waiting for the excitement. Larry Fender flew through the barn door. When he stood up, John Crane hit him again. Fender flew back another five feet. This time Fender only got to his knees before Man-Mountain hit him again. Fender fell straight back like he was shot. He didn't move. John Crane stood over him, then turned him over on his stomach, pulled out a wrist tie and bound his hands behind his back.

We dragged the others out of the house and lined them up on the dirt. I called Mark asking him to drive the Humvee to the house. Ben called 911 informing them of our location and circumstances.

With the culprits incapacitated, we walked into the barn and found the two girls lying in a pile of dirty straw, completely disheveled. Their faces were filthy and their clothes were torn. We untied them, gently pulled off the duct tape and they smiled for the first time in days. They couldn't believe that this version of hell was finally over.

"You're the guys from the gas station that tried to rescue us," Kelly said.

Jenni said, "We can't ever thank you enough. We were absolutely terrified. We thought we would never see our parents again."

"Both of you were very brave," I said

Words couldn't describe how happy they were. They hugged Ben and me as tight as they could, then the girls walked over and kicked Larry Fender again and again. Nobody even thought about stopping them.

I handed my phone to Jenni who immediately called her parents. Kelly was already talking to her mom on Ben's phone. Even though I'm a parent, I can't even begin to imagine the relief they felt hearing their daughters' voices.

It wasn't long before we could see police lights flashing in the distance.

"Here's where I get off. Not likely I'll ever see you again," John Crane said, looking me in the eyes.

I understood. He liked to live in the shadows, arriving from nowhere when the time was right and disappearing in an instant. He probably also didn't want to have to explain how an escaped convict ended up dead, with Crane's note and $200,000 in his pocket.

"Good luck and many thanks," was all I could think to say.

Chapter Fifteen

The authorities pulled up and Sargent Leven, the officer in charge, stepped out. They took our statements, a quizzical look on their faces as they wrote the preliminary information down. If I hadn't lived through it, I wouldn't have believed it either. They drove us to the Holiday Inn, feeling the weight of the world was off our shoulders. I could only imagine how the two girls felt. They would need a lot of counseling ahead. It was late. The girls took a room together. Ben, Mark and I made our way down the hall. A cot and extra bedding was delivered. Mark and Ben looked at each other.

"We'll flip a coin for the bed" Ben said, handing a coin to Mark. "You flip it and I'll call it. Fair enough?"

"Fair enough," Mark stated.

Mark tossed the coin in the air and Ben called "Heads". Mark caught the coin, flipping it onto the back of his hand. It was "Heads". Mark grumbled and took the cot. He pulled the blankets up and was asleep in seconds. Ben stretched out on one bed, making an exaggeratedly satisfied sound. I slipped into the other bed. Ben placed the coin on the night stand between our beds. I picked it up and saw that was a two headed coin. Ben looked at me, winking. I smiled as I closed my eyes.

I don't remember anything until Sargent Leven knocked on the door.

He asked if we would join him as soon as we were dressed. We met the girls, escorted by a female police officer, on the way to breakfast. Earlier that morning the female officer had stopped by a 24-hour box store and purchased some much needed clothing and personal supplies. The girls were cleaned up, comfortably dressed, and looking forward to breakfast.

After breakfast, we picked up our gear, checked out of the hotel, and were driven to the Laredo Police Department where we reviewed our statements. Sargent Leven told us that he heard from the prosecuting attorney that Larry Fender was going to be held without bond. The others would face charges, but would probably be allowed to leave after posting bail. Ace Wilson was in critical condition at a Laredo hospital and was not expected to live. He also told us that we would have to return for the grand jury in a few months.

We drove the girls to the airport and walked with them as far as we could. After another round of hugs, they were off. "Good luck. We'll see you in about a week. Say 'hello' to your parents," I said. After going through security, numerous officers would walk them to their gates and see them onto the plane.

We retraced our steps, picking up Mark's rental car at the Mister Donuts. We piled back into the Camaro and slowly wound our way back to Michigan. We had risked our lives and weathered more than one crisis to help two young girls whose parents we knew. That's what good neighbors do.

My phone rang.

"Hello Bill, I have good news." Sheriff Remington said. "Larry Fender is being held for murder, kidnapping, human trafficking across state lines, attempted murder, unlawful possession of a firearm, conspiracy, rape, sex abuse and credit card fraud."

"Wow! And what happened to Ace Wilson?"

"He died last night at the Laredo hospital. His death bed testimony implicating Fender should stand up in court," Sheriff Remington said. "The FBI has taken over jurisdiction in the case. Clare and Clyde Helmon are charged with a number of federal crimes, including aiding and abetting a kidnapping and human trafficking. The mother is charged with harboring known fugitives. They're going away for a long time. I will let you know when they need you to return for the trial. It won't be for several months. Talk to you in a few days," he said, disconnecting.

When we were within 10 miles of Victorious, I phoned ahead and heard more good news. We drove directly to the Victorious

Hospital and arrived just as Tyler was being released. His dad pushed the wheel chair and Carolyn and his mom walked along, one on each side, beaming at him. Tyler seemed to like that. John slapped us on the back with congratulations for a job well done and Valerie gave us a big hug.

The Sandersons and Durants pulled up next to us. They couldn't thank us enough for saving their daughters.

"These last few years have taught us some tough lessons," I said. "Life just isn't as simple as it was when we were growing up here in Victorious. The outside world has caught up to us and we have to be more vigilant than we used to be, especially when the kids come home for the *Fireworks on the Dead River.*

Part IV

Winter on the Dead River

Chapter One

We already had plenty of snow, the tree branches along the cross-country ski trail hung gracefully down, touching the ground; the air was clear and crisp. A dusting of new snow caused every tree branch to sparkle. It was perfectly quiet. The only sound we could hear was the shushing of our skis.

We crossed several sets of deer tracks. The deer usually lingered in the forest surrounding the Dead River until the snow got too deep; then, they migrated south where winters were easier. Maybe, they're smarter than we are.

We got a good workout shoveling the drifted snow away from the front door. Once inside, I started a fire and it wasn't long before the meat sauce was underway and the pasta was boiling. I lit the candles and turned the lights off.

"I packed some Stella Rosa. Would you like some wine? I asked.

"Sure," Barb answered. "And how about salad with the meal?"

"That would be great," I responded.

After the meal we cleaned up the kitchen and sat down on the couch, enjoying the view of the river. The water was frozen over, with ice thick enough for people to drill holes and fish and the occasional snowmobiler could race from one end of the river to the other.

I heard the door slam next door. It was our new neighbor, Carolyn Raft. She had purchased the property after the old Wylies cottage burned down the previous year. She has replaced it with a beautiful modular home. Carolyn worked as the county medical examiner and had settled in nicely in her new life in the Superior Peninsula, leaving a terrible marriage downstate behind and moving north to get a fresh start.

She did a great job and had helped us out with several previous cases. She and police officer Tyler Baldwin had first met during one of them. They were still seeing each other almost every day and. I wouldn't have been surprised if their engagement, or even a wedding date, were announced sometime soon.

The next morning, the thermometer read a balmy twenty degrees – perfect weather for skiing.

"Hey, Carolyn," I called as we skied past her driveway. She was shoveling the back stairs. "You going to the special ceremony to celebrate the arrival of the new county rescue helicopter later today?"

"Sure am," she replied. "It's a great day for Mesabi County. See you there!"

A few doors down, we skied by our old friend, Kenny Bievins. Kenny was out moving snow with a new plow truck. He was probably the only person on the Dead River who looked forward to new snow.

"Are you going to the early Mass?" Kenny Bievins asked.

"Yep, right after the celebration for the new helicopter!" we replied.

"Great!" he continued. "It looks like we're starting the Christmas season early this year with caroling before church, and hot chocolate and treats in the activity center later," Kenny said.

"That sounds like fun. We'll see you there," Barb said.

On the return leg of the ski trail, we passed Dennis St. Amour, who had just finished clearing his driveway. He had the misfortune to be a Detroit Lions fan. Dwight Eisenhower was president the last time they won the National Football League championship. Most people in Mesabi County favored the Green Bay Packers; now there was a team to root for! They'd won a number of championships and were in it until the end almost every year.

"Hey Denny!" I called. "How about the Packers? You know that people were still driving Edsels the last time the Lions were good," I said.

"It's easy to root for a winning team, but it takes character to be a Lion's fan. We expect to lose. Victory is always a pleasant surprise," Dennis said.

"Well spoken," Barb put in. "Are you going to see the new rescue helicopter this afternoon?"

"I think we can make it," Dennis said.

Barb and I waved and headed back. After a relaxing hour in the sauna, it was time to get back to reality.

Chapter Two

Mesabi County had waited decades, and the voters finally approved a bond last year to cover the cost of a rescue helicopter. That afternoon, at a grand celebration in front of the Mesabi County Courthouse, the helicopter was unveiled. The local politicians made speeches and everyone wanted to get their picture taken next to the helicopter.

The pilot was Deputy Roads. He had flown helicopters in the service and, with 150 hours of additional training, he could really put it through its paces. Not only was he the most qualified of the applicants, he had also been injured in the course of an investigation last year, and getting helicopter duty was a reward for service beyond the call of duty. He was the perfect choice for the position and we were excited that he was chosen. He was equally excited to be the first pilot.

Among the large and festive crowd, only one person had a sour look on his face – Carolyn's fellow county employee, Don Dempster. Although Don had made countless attempts to win her affection, she had always politely, but firmly turned down his invitations to have coffee together at work, or to hit the bars together on the weekend.

Dempster felt he had a lot more to offer than that Needleton police sergeant, Tyler Baldwin. Just seeing Carolyn with Baldwin at the celebration turned his stomach.

As the crowd thinned, Dempster struck up a conversation with Deputy Roads. "You excited to fly that helicopter?" Dempster asked. "She's a beauty."

"Yeah!" Deputy Roads answered. "She can really dance… so easy to maneuver. We'll have no problem getting into tight spots in the woods, or on the back roads now."

"When will you take her up?"

"I'm giving Carolyn a ride tomorrow. She wants to fly over the Dead River and see her cottage from the air. She asked Tyler to come along. I've got space for you, too. Want to come?" Deputy Roads asked.

"Can't tomorrow," Don Dempster responded. "Maybe next week some time?"

Walking away, Don hatched the perfect plan. If he could just monkey around with the helicopter, he could eliminate Tyler and get his revenge on Carolyn at the same time. He would sneak into the hanger at the Mesabi International Airport and loosen a few things, maybe the rear tail rotor? It would still take off just fine, but after a while, Deputy Roads would lose control, and they'd spin out and crash. No way to prove foul play. It was basically a maiden flight and anything could happen. The helicopter had already been inspected; the chances, of another inspection, between tonight and tomorrow were zero.

Covering his license plate with duct tape and then packing snow on top of that, he was sure that his vehicle couldn't be identified, that is, if anyone even noticed. Pulling his hood up and putting on a ski mask, Dempster stepped inside the fence and proceeded confidently, but quietly, to the hangar. He grabbed some tools from the work bench, snagged the step ladder next to it, and went to work, loosening the bolts on the lower swash plate. It would only be a matter of time before the lower and upper plates would become disconnected.

Quietly carrying the stepladder back to its original position, he heard a noise. It was the night watchman, Tony Marten, making his rounds. Marten shined the flashlight around the hanger, missing Dempster who was flat on the floor over in the corner behind some 50-gallon barrels, but spotting the wrench Dempster had left on the floor. Thinking nothing of it, Marten walked over, picked it and placed it back on the work bench among the other odds and ends. Dempster waited, then crawled out of his hiding place, placed the wrench back on its hook, cautiously opened the door and slipped out, looking back over his shoulder at the helicopter. "Enjoy the ride, Carolyn. It will be a memorable one for all of us."

Chapter Three

It was gently snowing as we arrived at the church and the caroling really brought the spirit of Christmas alive for both singers and listeners alike.

"Are all of your children and grandchildren coming for Christmas?" Betty Durant asked me.

"Yes, and we can't wait. It will be the first time in a year we will sit down together. I miss the grandchildren very much," Barb said. "I bet you're especially thankful this Christmas, having your daughter back."

Betty turned to me and said, "Indeed we are… and I know the Sandersons are too. We can't thank you and your friends enough for what you did last summer."

"I'd just be happy with a Lions victory this week," Dennis St. Amour said.

'I don't think even God can perform that miracle," I said.

Chapter Four

Carolyn rose early and called "Are you sure you can't go with me?"

"Not a chance; with other officers taking off for the holidays, I have to take a shift," Tyler replied. "Have fun, though! I'll be watching the skies! Love you!"

"Right back at you," Carolyn responded.

Carolyn drove to Mesabi International Airport and met Deputy Roads inside the hangar.

"I am really looking forward to this. Do you think we can still fly over my house on the Dead River? I'd love to see it from the air."

"No problem. The weather is perfect and the visibility is great," Deputy Roads replied. "Let's do this!"

He eased the helicopter out of the hangar, then Carolyn watched as he slowly opened the throttle, gradually pulled the Collective, pushed the left pedal down, and pushed the Cyclic forward. From Carolyn's perspective, the whole incomprehensible process was like magic! They were off. Viewing the winding path of the Dead River and then seeing her new house from above was incredible.

Suddenly, the helicopter began to shudder. The front end dropped and the back started to swerve. Andy Roads had lived through a number of close calls flying helicopters when he was in the service, but this was over the top. Something was seriously wrong. "When I say 'Jump,' open your door and bail out! Think *feet, thigh, hip, back and roll, and* then run like hell," Deputy Roads screamed.

The helicopter was making wide circles, as it dropped lower and lower all on its own; he had totally lost control. Quickly calculating where it would finally crash onto the ice and explode, he waited until they were about 30 feet in the air, over the trees and shoreline, low enough that hopefully they wouldn't be killed on impact, but far enough away from the explosion to have a chance at survival. "Now," he bellowed. "Carolyn! Get out now!" Seconds later and not more than 200 feet away, the helicopter nosedived onto the ice and exploded.

Looking out our window, we couldn't believe the inferno. A plume of black smoke rose high above the river, alerting neighbors from the West End all the way down to the dam. I called 911. Minutes later, snowmobiles, some pulling sleds laden with anything anyone thought they might need, began to appear, sending up huge clouds of puffy snow as they blasted through the 5 foot drifts and fish-tailed as they raced along on the ice.

As the immediate blast began to die back, the observers began to draw nearer. Barb and I joined in, wading through the waist deep snow along the shoreline to join the search. In our haste, we forgot to grab our snowshoes.

"Over there," I yelled, pointing down toward the shore just down from our cottage. "There's something over there!"

A snowmobile headed our way, pausing just long enough for me to jump on behind the driver. Another swooped up Barb and we were off.

Deputy Roads had fallen over a cluster of majestic white pines. They must have been mere seedlings when the last great lumbering effort had taken place along the Dead River. Not especially bushy, they didn't exactly provide a soft landing, but they broke his fall. He slipped through the soft upper branches, then bounced and banged off the larger ones below until he finally fell the last 15 feet to the drifted snow below.

Carolyn had not been so lucky. She had dropped right into the snowdrift that rose up the bank from the ice to the high flat jack pine forest beyond

We could hear sirens – Sheriff Remington arrived followed by the Victorious and Needleton emergency vehicles. Providentially, the Campers' Board had worked with the various county executives to establish a system of property identification signs. It made pinpointing the exact location on the many winding woodland roads a lot faster and easier in times of crisis. The Victorious fire trucks followed. Since the tank truck could only carry 700 gallons of water, volunteers used an ice auger to drill a hole in the ice and the firefighters dropped the hose from the pumping truck through. Fortunately, they had access to the river; now they could suck up enough water to maintain the high-pressure stream flowing.

Having heard about the accident on the police scanner, Tyler Baldwin rushed to the scene. His walk turned into a jog and then a sprint as he raced down the shoreline. He fell to his knees as they stabilized Carolyn on a backboard and then joined in as they carried her as fast as they could to the waiting emergency vehicle.

The EMTs were already loading a battered, but conscious Andy Roads into the ambulance.

Mark and Ben arrived, then John Baldwin and his wife; within an hour, it seemed that half the town of Victorious had heard about the accident and had somehow gotten themselves to the scene. Don Dempster was part of the ever-growing crowd. "Now that was an explosion," he whispered. He had especially enjoyed watching Tyler slip and slide his way across the ice, then fall to his knees, sobbing, as the EMTs finished strapping Carolyn in.

"The M.E. says he won't be able to confirm if there were others in the 'copter for days. At least Deputy Roads and Carolyn got out before it exploded, although their prognosis can't be good," Sheriff Remington said.

Returning to the cottage, my son Joe wondered aloud what caused the crash.

"It was the first flight. It could have been a mechanical problem," I said. "Although the thing was brand new and had just been inspected."

The Federal Aviation Administration had a team on site the next morning. They secured the entire area and examined the debris, looking for obvious causes like an incendiary device, or a fuel leak. With a crane, they lifted the largest pieces of the debris onto a flatbed, and then cleaned up even the smallest fragments. They made sure that nothing would fall into the river when the ice melted in the spring.

Chapter Five

The Mining Ledger assumed it was mechanical failure, but a week had passed and there was no confirmation from the FAA that the newspaper's explanation was correct. The manufacturer had sent several of their experts to examine the debris, too, hoping to find that the crash was due to pilot error.

I entered the sheriff's department hoping to find answers.

"Good morning, "I said to the sheriff".

"I can only imagine what bring you to my office," Sheriff Remington said,   "Let me help you out. Neither the FAA, nor the manufacturer had come up with a firm understanding of what had happened. "We may never know."

"Do you mind if the guys and I look into it?" I asked.

Sheriff Remington replied, "Just stay on the right side of the law. Your little birdie is out of commission; I know that she was leading you old goats along."

I said, "But Strom, we did obtain justice in every one of the cases."

"Get out before I throw you out," he concluded.

The following Monday night, we convened as usual at *Geno's Pizzeria.* Even Tyler was there.

Tyler led off the conversation: "First off, Carolyn's still in a coma, but at least things aren't getting any worse. Now, does anybody know who would have a grudge against either her or Deputy Roads?"

"Mark and I can check with her co-workers," Ben Myers said.

"I can check her house. I've got a key to the front door," Tyler said.

"John and I will look for a mechanic who can really look over the remains of the helicopter, although I can't imagine that the

FAA and manufacturer's team missed too much." I said.

The next day Tyler drove to Carolyn's cottage. It was eerie being at Carolyn's cottage without her. He hoped she'd be home soon, but it had only been a week since the accident.

He opened the top drawer and thumbed through them. Part way down, he found her Last Will and Testament and beneath that, her life insurance policy. He put both documents in his pocket.

Since they shared the same password, he quickly accessed her files. Finding nothing of interest, he turned to her e-mail, opening up any messages that looked relevant. Clicking on the trash icon brought hundreds of emails onto the screen. Most of them were spam, but several stood out. They were from *Mesabiplayboy1975*. Unable to resist he opened the first one. It was dated a year ago:

> *Carolyn, I would like to see you. Would you like to have a drink tonight at Reflections? I will see you at work.*

Each subsequent message became more aggressive, and none of them were signed. The most recent was dated one month ago:

> *Carolyn, I don't know what you see in Baldwin. He doesn't love you like I do. I can give you everything. I won't take "no" for an answer.*

Interestingly, they were all sent from a server at the Mesabi Sheriff's department. It shouldn't be hard to have a geek trace them back to the sender.

John and I were having coffee at Millie's. "I think I know a helicopter mechanic who might be able to help. He retired from the Air Force some years ago. I play cribbage with him every once in a while when I visit the VA home. I will give him a call. His name is Jerry Langley."

"That sounds great. Count me in," I said.

When we picked him up the next morning, he had a big smile on his face – he was looking forward to the adventure and was happy to be getting out of the VA for a day.

"Hello, Jerry," John said. "This is Bill Bennet. We're trying to figure out if the helicopter crash on the Dead River a couple weeks ago was an accident."

Jerry said, "I can take a look. I can't guarantee anything."

As we approached the hangar, the security guard, Tony Marten, came over and said, "Nobody is allowed in the hanger. It's restricted."

"Not even for an old sheriff," I said smiling.

He smiled, and we shook hands.

"Just don't make trouble," Tony said.

We entered the hanger and Jerry said, "Well, it was an EC-135," And bring me some tools." After 20 minutes of poking and prying, Jerry stated: "The Fenestron system is like a protective shield. Even in a crash, it would have protected the interior of the rotor. But it's all burned up inside. Someone definitely loosened the shield. I'd stake my reputation on it. I worked on these all my life," Jerry said.

We had our answer.

Meanwhile, Mark and Ben entered the Sheriff's Department and approached two people in white coats who were chatting in the hallway. "Excuse me, but we're trying to find someone who knew Carolyn Raft. Can you point us in the right direction?" Mark Kestila asked.

"You might try Don Dempster. He was always following her around."

"Where will we find him?" Ben asked.

"He works on the third floor. He is our forensic expert."

"Thanks," Mark replied. Then turning to Ben, in a quiet voice he continued: "See, Ben you just have to be nice and people will help you out. "

"Shut up," Ben Myers said.

They approached the elevator; the sign on the doors read *Out of Order.*

You mean I have to walk up to the third floor?" Mark asked.

"I am certainly not going to carry you," Ben replied with a smile. They ambled up the stairway.

They knocked on the door marked *Forensics, and* then entered.

"My name is Ben Myers and this is Mark Kestila. Are you Don Dempster?" I asked.

He nodded. "We're talking to some of Carolyn's co-workers to see if that sheds any light on the accident," Ben said.

"She was really a very nice person. We all hope that she'll pull through. Terrible accident," Don Dempster said.

"That's just it. We're not sure it was an accident," Ben said.

"Really?" Don said in surprise. "I don't believe anyone would hurt Carolyn. I didn't see much of her... just when I visited her laboratory downstairs, or when she brought me something to examine up here. She was the nicest person I knew," Don said.

Ben asked, "But do you know of someone who might have wanted to hurt her?"

Dempster said, "I can't imagine it. You might want to check with her co-workers down in the lab."

"So I'm hearing that you didn't know her very well, or see her outside of work," Ben stated.

"Correct," Dempster replied. "I'm a confirmed bachelor."

"Thanks for your time," Mark said.

Even after questioning Carolyn's colleagues and mentioning their hunch to anyone who would listen, they learned nothing new.

"I think these people know more than they are letting on," Mark stated, as they left the building.

"Gotta be careful now," Dempster thought to himself. Using an "eraser" program that he downloaded, he encrypted the files on his hard drive, and then entered new data. No one would ever be able to find his server address now.

Chapter Six

The team reconvened at *Geno's Pizzeria*. Tyler Baldwin couldn't wait to tell us that he had found Carolyn's will, her life insurance policy, and some threatening emails from *Mesabiplayboy1975* on her computer. "I got a buddy who can check the server address to see where they came from," he concluded.

John weighed in: "Bill and I took an old friend who is living in the VA home out to Mesabi International Airport. He worked for years on helicopters in the Air Force. He swears that the tail rotor was tampered with," John Baldwin said.

"Wonder how the FAA missed that?" Ben said, with a puzzled look.

Then Mark added: "But we didn't find out much at the Sheriff's Department. We're going back tomorrow."

We continued discussing the case. The bar owner, Rick Bonnettelli, just kept smiling and kept the beer coming.

The next morning, Mark and Ben drove back to the sheriff's department and went straight down to the lab.

"Excuse us. We're trying to find someone who knew Carolyn Raft." Mark Kestila shared with the young man sitting at a desk.

He replied, "I really didn't know Carolyn very well. I just started working here. I'm Chris Maxwell. I just got my discharge from the Air Force last month."

"You haven't seen, or heard anything out of the usual, though, have you?" Ben asked.

After a pause and a quick look around to see who was listening, he said: "Well... Don Dempster from Forensics used to come down here a lot. It didn't seem like he really needed anything; he just wanted to chat with Carolyn."

"Thanks," Ben said. "That really helps."

"Mark, we're going to get our exercise today."

"What do you mean?"

"We have to talk to Don Dempster. It's only four flights of stairs from way down here. All that cardio will make you feel like a new man," Ben teased.

Mark huffed and puffed up the stairs to the Forensics Department and knocked on the door.

"Come in," Don Dempster called.

"Hello again," Ben said. "We're back ... and we heard something that doesn't quite line up with what you told us. Someone told us that you actually used to look for reasons to hang around the lab and chat with Carolyn."

"Where did you hear such a thing?" Don Dempster asked.

Ben said, "It appears to be all over the Sheriff's Department."

"Well, they're just plain wrong," Dempster shot back. "I only saw her professionally, on official business, and I don't like where this conversation is going. Get out."

After they exited, Ben looked at Mark and said, "Well, we lit a fire under him. We'll see what it produces."

On the other side of town Tyler had contacted an old school friend who owned a computer business in Victorious.

"How are you doing?" Tyler asked as he entered *Cam's Computer Sales and Service.*

"Been hanging around; spending way too much time keeping the business going, but in spite of the big box stores, I am thankful that the locals need their stuff cleaned, or repaired and the older folks always need a lesson or two," Cam said. "So what's up?"

"Police business, actually. I am trying to locate a server. Can you find where the address *Mesabiplayboy1975* originated?"

"It will take some time, but I'll give it a try," Cam said.

"Thanks. Give me a call when you find out," Tyler called as he closed the door behind him.

Several hours had passed and Dempster was growing more and more worried about covering his tracks. Switching back to his old user he saw that it was being tracked, but two can play at that game, he thought. Following the tracking agent through its Simple Mail Transfer Protocol (SMTP), he pulled the address up on his screen. He'd pay that computer geek a visit on his lunch hour.

I just couldn't reconcile the FAA's statement that the cause of the crash was inconclusive with John's buddy's verdict of foul play. I went back to the Mesabi Airport and found Tony Marten.

"Hey Tony," I said as I approached him. "Do you remember anything unusual about the night before the helicopter crash?" I asked.

Tony Marten thought for a moment. "Not really. There was a wrench on the floor that I picked up and put back on the work bench, but otherwise it was 'all quiet' as usual."

"Let's see if you could find that wrench again." I suggested.

"Let's take a look," Tony Marten said.

It took him no time to find it. He pointed out the distinctive chip in one end.

"You mind if I take this with me?" I asked, promising to return it as soon as possible. I will return it," I said. I called Tyler. Tony and I rehashed the local news until Tyler arrived. He slipped the wrench into an evidence bag and dropped it off at the Mesabi sheriff's office to be dusted for prints.

Chapter Seven

Rocky's Bar was dark and filled with people whose dreams were still waiting to come true. Carolyn Raft's former husband, Craig Raft, was having a drink at the bar when Don Dempster walked in.

"You satisfied?" Don Dempster asked. "I won't be satisfied until she's dead," Raft said, "At least she still hasn't replaced me as the beneficiary on her life insurance policy – tough to do when you're in the ICU. I hadn't even thought about her getting remarried... and we couldn't let that happen, could we? Like I told you, 50/50 split on a cool one million dollars." He continued: "And that pay-off is looking better and better what with the FAA's verdict. Now don't you go doing anything stupid. You gotta play the grieving co-worker who misses her the most. Just go to work and act normal. And don't contact me again."

"Yeah, I know. I know. But those old geezers are snooping around, and Baldwin's got a computer geek trying to find my server. Those emails I sent will be big trouble if they fall into the wrong hands. The geek's going down tonight," Dempster said.

"Just do it," Craig Raft said.

Dempster left the bar; nobody even looked up. Then and there, Raft decided that Dempster had become a loose end.

Chapter Eight

Sitting at my kitchen table with a cup of coffee, I read over the papers that Tyler had given me. In the will, she had listed her former husband as her sole beneficiary and the accidental death benefit was a million bucks. Seemed like a pretty good motive to me. It was time to call the life insurance company.

After working my way through an assortment of menus, I was impressed when a real person answered.

"Hello. I am calling regarding policy GL353566575778."

"Are you the beneficiary?" The agent asked.

"No, I'm just checking regarding the procedure the company pays out to the beneficiary".

"Well, in general, upon verification of death from the county medical examiner, it usually takes seven to ten business days for the check to be mailed," the agent said.

"Thank you," I replied. We definitely had a line on a new suspect, and he had the best possible motive.

Tyler's friend Cam was in the back room of his computer shop trying to trace the email address Tyler had asked him to locate. He heard the front office door open and close. Cam said, "Hello, who's there?" There was no response.

Cam came out of the back room and immediately felt a thump on the back of his head. Don Dempster hit him a few more times to make sure the job was done, and then dragged the body into the back room. After that kind of a beating, no way the kid could survive. He pressed the DVD security camera *open* button and put the CD in his pocket, then, just to be sure the kid was out of the way, he lit a cigarette and dropped it into the waste basket. He had made maximum use of his lunch hour and would be seen at his desk when the news of the fire broke.

Fortunately for Cam, the town of Victorious is not very big and the central fire station is not more than three blocks away from any of the downtown establishments. They were on the scene within minutes of the time a passer-by had smelled smoke coming out of the old brick building. By the time Tyler drove up, firefighters were spraying water through the front windows and the rescue team had already entered the building from the rear, carefully, but quickly carrying the unconscious proprietor out of the back workroom and into the waiting ambulance.

Tyler immediately began putting two and two together. His request for information was certainly the impetus for this attack.

As Remington was watching the fire intently, Tyler walked over to him and said, "That man may die because I asked him to do me a favor. I found some questionable emails on Carolyn's computer and asked Cam to find the origin for the server. Whoever did this really doesn't want to be found. It looks like the crash really wasn't an accident."

"What do you mean by that?" Sheriff Remington asked.

"My dad and Bill Bennett took an expert helicopter mechanic out to the hangar. He maintains the tail rotor was tampered with, which means it wasn't an accident," Tyler added.

"Why didn't you tell me this?" Sheriff Remington barked.

"We needed proof. You probably wouldn't have believed us," Tyler said.

"I believe you now," Sheriff Remington said, "Have your dad and his half-wit detective friends meet me in my office in one hour." Sheriff Remington got into his cruiser and drove away.

"Hey, Bill! It's Tyler. Sheriff Remington wants us to meet with him in one hour in his office. He's not at all pleased that we haven't shared our updates with him."

I said, "I'll call the others."

Gathered in Sheriff Remington's office, we felt like school kids who had been called to the principal's office. He sat glaring at us.

Remington started the conversation by asking, "Do you know how stupid you are?"

"Is that rhetorical or a real question?" I asked, trying to break the tension.

Remington said, "A man is in the critical care unit because you didn't come to me and tell me what you knew."

"In our defense, you have not actually been very receptive to our investigations in the past and have repeatedly told us to lay off and stay out of the proceedings. We're sure you would not have believed us if we told you the helicopter was tampered with, particularly since the FAA didn't find any evidence to support that claim. You've always harped on us about having evidence. What's the evidence? Well, we were waiting until we had evidence before we came to you," I said.

"You should have told me," Sheriff Remington bellowed.

"Not so fast," I cautioned in a defiant tone. "The threatening e-mails that Carolyn received were sent through the county server. It could have been any employee doing that. For that matter, it could have been you. We couldn't trust anyone," Tyler said.

"I should lock all of you up and throw away the key," Sheriff Remington growled.

There was total silence. The best thing we could do was just sit there and shut up. But Tyler was right. We couldn't trust anyone using the county computer server.

"I'll call the FAA back to re-examine the helicopter debris. If the tail rotor has been tampered with, they will find it. Now get out," Sheriff Remington snarled.

We walked out like five kids leaving the whipping shed.

Raft worried about loose ends and Dempster certainly was one; and better yet, he'd believe anything. Raft phoned Dempster and said, "Hello, Dempster! Let's meet out at the old 510 steel bridge. A sizeable amount of money came through to cover family needs while Carolyn is out of commission. I've got your share."

Dempster replied, "I suppose, but it's awful cold to be meeting in such a remote place. I'm not staying long."

Craig Raft was waiting on the 510 Bridge when Don Dempster

pulled up and stepped out of his car. He asked, "And tell me again why you wanted to meet out here. Couldn't you just give it to me in *Rocky's Bar?*"

"Nobody will disturb us; besides, it's a large amount of dough that I've got in the back seat," Raft continued, "It's in my briefcase."

As Raft opened the passenger side back door, Dempster walked over. Reversing direction, Raft grabbed Dempster's coat with both hands and threw him over the bridge. There was a thud when the body smashed onto the frozen river below. He then walked over to Dempster's car, stepped in, and drove it to the edge. Leaving the transmission in drive, Raft applied pressure on the accelerator, stepping away from the automobile and watching with satisfaction as it careened over the edge. It crashed onto the ice into the Dead River. It looked like someone had taken the corner too fast and gone through the rail. No need to share the money with Dempster now. No loose ends.

Chapter Nine

At the sheriff's department I climbed the stairs to the forensics laboratory, knocked, then entered.

"You must be new here," I said. "I used to be the sheriff before Remington. My name is Bill Bennett."

"John Washburn," he said, shaking my hand. "I was actually hired about a year ago, but I usually work in the annex. I'm here today because our main forensics expert didn't come in to work. We don't know where he is."

"Don Dempster?" I asked. I remembered that Mark and Ben had mentioned his name. "Thanks anyway," I answered, as I left.

With his buddy, Cam, still in intensive care, Tyler decided to drop by the computer repair store in Needleton. Tyler had helped the store owner when he was accused of selling stolen merchandise. Tyler had testified on his behalf, pleading for leniency and probation and the judge had concurred. The guy definitely owed Tyler Baldwin a favor. He pulled up in front of *Computers Galore* and stepped into the store.

"Hello, Rick," Tyler said

"Well, to what do I owe the pleasure?" Rick asked.

"I need a favor. I'm trying to track down some intimidating emails that were sent to my girlfriend by someone called Mesabiplayboy1975. To be square with your, I have to tell you someone almost killed the previous computer expert I asked to do this, then set his store on fire. He's in intensive care right now. If you don't want to do this, I totally understand."

Rick replied "Hey. You saved my life by talking to the judge. I owe you everything, I will do anything and I am always ready for trouble." He whistled and a Doberman pinscher walked out from the back room.

Tyler smiled.

"Give me a couple of hours and I will get back to you," Rick said.

Shaking Rick's hand, Tyler walked out, keeping a keen eye on the dog.

Having completed his mission at the old steel bridge, Craig Raft showed up at *Rocky's*. He had just sat down at the bar when the bar tender asked where his buddy was.

"I think he took a trip," Raft replied.

Chapter Ten

Dempster crawled as best he could; he had to make it to the road in case a car passed by, although he knew that most of the traffic these days took the new bridge. Staying alive long enough to take out Craig Raft was all that kept him going.

The next morning, Tyler was getting dressed when his IPhone rang. Tyler said, "Hello." It was Rick. He had traced the email address to a county server which was located on the third floor of the Sheriff's Department. Mesabiplayboy1975 belonged to Don Dempster.

"Great job, I appreciate it very much," Tyler said.

"Anytime you need a favor, call me, OK?" Rick said.

I was fast asleep when my cell phone rang. It was Tyler. He said, " Hello, I just off the phone with a computer friend. He traced the threatening e-mails back to Don Dempster."

"Thanks," I said as I disconnected and closed my eyes.

My cell phone rang again. "My, you're popular this morning," Barb said. I picked it up and heard, "Mr. Bennett? This is John Washburn… the technician from the sheriff's department? Sheriff Remington said it was all right to let you know that I checked the wrench for fingerprints and it is clean."

"Okay, thanks. I appreciate it very much," I said.

As evidence, it wasn't admissible in court, but I had a hunch somebody made sure there were no fingerprints on it. My instincts told me it was Don Dempster.

"It's all coming together, Barb," I said.

There was work to do and no time for sleep. I showered and dressed, then called the team – we'd meet at *Millies* in half an hour.

Mark and Ben were the first to arrive. They were already

on their second cup of coffee when I walked in. John Baldwin entered right behind me. Tyler would join us as soon as he could.

"Here is what we know. Tyler gave the wrench to Don Dempster. We don't know if Dempster examined the wrench, but the wrench came up clean. Tyler had a friend, Cam, try and locate the server for Mesabiplayboy1975. Cam was beaten within an inch of his life, left for dead, and his business burned down around him. Tyler immediately called in a favor from another friend who traced the e-mails back to Dempster, and Dempster didn't show up for work yesterday. I think we can make an assumption Dempster is involved," I said. "And either he's flown, or he's dead. I also read Carolyn's will and her former husband is the sole beneficiary if Carolyn dies. Craig Raft stands to inherit one million dollars if the FAA report holds up. Unfortunately, we have no proof to tie him to the crime."

Tyler burst into the restaurant. "Carolyn came out of the coma and is making eye contact and moving her arms and legs.

"That's great!" I said. Soon everyone in *Millie's* was smiling, and then phoning anyone they could think of to share the news.

When things settled down, Tyler added: "They found Don Dempster near the 510 steel bridge. He's unconscious and half frozen to death. They took him to the Victorious Hospital."

When we arrived at the ER, EMTs were performing CPR; a nurse covered Dempster with warming blankets; another hooked up a heart monitor and a cuff while a third inserted oxygen tubes into his nose. Doctor Bell entered the room, looked at us, and said, "Go back to the waiting room."

The sheriff entered the E.R. and was already up to speed. "I hope Dempster pulls through. He probably knows the whole story," he said.

Several hours passed. We learned that Dempster had regained consciousness briefly, but was incoherent. His core temperature wasn't coming up, and they had placed him on life support.

An hour or two later, Dr. Bell emerged again and asked, "Does Mr. Dempster have any family?"

We didn't know.

"Go home, boys. We'll keep an eye on him," Sheriff Remington said.

I was too tired to disagree. As we were heading out, Doctor Bell re-emerged. "So sorry to share bad news, but Mr. Dempster didn't make it. There was nothing more we could do."

After a pause, Sheriff Remington said, "And now we have no witness."

"Maybe we do," I told the team. "We have to find Craig Raft before he hears about Dempster's demise."

Tyler Baldwin immediately left the Emergency Room, his dad right behind him. They sped out of the parking lot and disappeared. Tyler thought he knew where Raft might be hiding.

Ben, Mark, and I decided to visit some of the local watering holes. Suffice to say we had no luck.

Chapter Eleven

As they approached Carolyn's cottage, Tyler flipped the head lights off and parked on the road. He removed his Glock and headed toward the house. His father followed a few feet behind. Peeking in the window, they saw Raft watching television. They knew they only had a short time before the local news came on. There was sure to be something on the news about the accident.

Tyler motioned for John to break the window. Tyler would immediately shoot through the opening. At the sound of breaking glass, Raft dived to the floor. Tyler shouted, *"Don't Move!"* He fired once, then smashed the rest of the window and dove through. By the time John got inside, the wrestling match was over. Tyler had gotten the upper hand. John grabbed his son and pulled him off.

"I'm going to kill you," Tyler promised, holding his gun to Raft's head.

Raft said, "It was all Dempster's idea. He planned the whole thing. I've got e-mails to prove it."

"Just shut up and sit over there. Don't move a muscle, or I'll let my son pound you to a pulp," John ordered.

Raft sat down on the floor quickly.

John called Sheriff Remington. "We're at Carolyn's cottage and we've got her ex-husband. He says Dempster planned the whole scheme."

"We'll be right there. Just hold on," Sheriff Remington said.

John called Mark and he, in turn, called Ben and me. We arrived right after Sheriff Remington and his deputies. "You should have allowed Tyler to beat him to death," Mark said.

One of the deputies handcuffed Raft, read him his rights,

secured him in one of the police cruisers, and left with his flashers on.

Chapter Twelve

We reconvened at *Geno's Pizzeria*. When the whole story came out, it was Raft who contacted Dempster to find out what his ex-wife was up to. In subsequent e-mails, it became apparent that Raft was only worried that she would get involved with someone else and replace him as her beneficiary. Dempster said that he could arrange an "accident", but it would cost Raft half of the insurance money. All Raft had to do was show up.

"It never would have worked," Ben said. "Remington told me that the FAA re-examined the wreckage and agreed with Jerry. The tail rotor had been tampered with."

"Yeah," John added. "The good news is that the insurance company is going to pay for a new helicopter. By the time it arrives, Andy Roads will be raring to go."

Mark jumped in: "And Raft's going to prison for a long time."

"I still should have killed him," Tyler said.

"What I want to know is how you knew Raft was staying at Carolyn's cottage," I said.

"When I stopped at her cottage the other day, I noticed gum wrappers in the waste basket. She's OCD. There's never anything in her wastebaskets," Tyler said.

"And how's her rehab coming along?" I asked.

"Better than anyone expected. It won't be long before she's back on her snowmobile cruising up and down the Dead River, blasting through snow drifts and fish-tailing on the ice!"

"Amen to that!" I exclaimed. "This will be a truly unforgettable *Winter on the Dead River*.

Part V

Revenge on the Dead River

Chapter One

It was great to see families reunited to enjoy chatting with friends as we passed each other in our boats, when stopping by for a cold brew, or when gathered around one of the campfires that sparkled along the shoreline at night. The singing was usually off key and stories were embellished over time, but, from one generation to the next, the roasted marshmallows and hot dogs were always perfect. Even when children left the area to pursue their careers, they cherished their visits home. The Dead River brings out the best in everyone. This heritage is one of the few things we can pass on to the next generation. As fast as the pace of the world has increased, life on the Dead River has remained constant.

Chapter Two

Larry Fender wasn't thinking about how glorious life was on the Dead River. He could only think of getting even with Bill Bennett. Bennett and his team had put an end to Fender's human trafficking racket, landing him in Federal Correctional Institution, in Milan, MI. After several months, he had run across a father-son duo, Wendel and Beau Wylie, who were also sentenced to the same hellhole thanks to the efforts of the same team of amateur detectives for making and selling meth in the Superior Peninsula,. Escape and revenge were always on their minds. During their one hour of free time each day, they plotted and planned.

While one might think that they literally had a lifetime to develop the perfect plan, time was actually running short. A new faction within the prison – *La Eme* (Mexican Mafia) – was fighting to take control from the Aryan Brotherhood, which had controlled the prison for twenty years. Both factions were led by brilliant, but dangerous individuals: Andres Lobo and Apolinar Rocio led *La Eme* while the AB countered with Bull Carlito and Brutus Holt. A prisoner had to pick a side, or risk certain death.

Wendel Wylie said, "We gotta get out of here pronto, or we'll be butchered in the gang war."

"Yeah," Beau Wylie confirmed. "I heard a gang started an electrical fire in an Ohio prison a few years ago just to get things going, and then took out a bunch of guards and most of their opponents."

Larry Fender added cautiously, "But many have tried, but almost none have succeeded. If we fail, it's solitary confinement for life."

"Are you afraid?" Beau Wylie challenged.

Hold on, Beau. We're better off doing this together. We just need to figure out how to get some rubber material and throw together something that looks like firemen's gear. When the fire breaks out, we mingle with the rescuers and then ride right out of here."

Larry Fender said, "I can handle that. Kitchen supplies are delivered in mega plastic-wrapped bulk loads. I'll stash up as much as I can."

Wendel Wylie said, "I'll figure out where to start the fire. Beau, you get working on the escape route. It'd be best if we could commandeer our own vehicle."

After taking an oath of secrecy, they went their separate ways.

Wendel lagged behind as the inmates moved from place to place. First thing, he noticed that the main electrical wires were encased in conduit and kept off limits behind a locked gate in close proximity to the guards' monitoring station. Starting an electrical fire there would be tough.

Fender began amassing small pieces of black plastic wrap, and then snatched bits of yellow caution tape that a construction company used to cordon off access to the chapel while repair work was being done.

Chapter Three

A few days later, Brutus Holt and Bull Carlito, leaders of the Aryan Brotherhood, paid the three of them a courtesy visit as they were walking in the courtyard during free time. "You boys haven't joined the AB," Holt said.

Carlito added, "Stir will go a lot easier if you're with us. You don't join, you'll in your cell waiting to be rescued, or risk certain death at the hand of *La Eme*."

"Besides your protection during this so-called riot, what's in it for us?" Wendel Wylie asked.

"We can get you work in whatever department you want," Holt replied, "but you have to make it through the initiation first. We'll be waiting for you at Cell Block D, 2nd floor tomorrow during the break. Be there, or we'll take that as a refusal," Brutus Holt said as he and Bull Carlito walked away.

"Those guys are nuts," Larry Fender said.

"Agreed, but we have no choice. It's one group of nut cases, or the other," Wendel Wylie said. Larry and Beau agreed.

The next day they showed up as ordered, were hooded, and beaten. It was the AB's way of testing their loyalty, and also reinforcing what would happen if they tried to leave the gang. The following day, a guy who was covered in tattoos, used a homemade ink gun to draw the Aryan Brotherhood logo, *Death before Dishonor"* on their backs.

The next morning, a slip of paper was slid under Beau Wylie's cell doors noting that he was re-assigned as the librarian's assistant. His job involved scanning books being checked in and out. Boring as hell, but he got unlimited use of the library's computer as well as access to supplies, like rubber cement and scissors. All three benefits would help further their plan.

That night Wendel Wylie ordered, "Beau, get friendly with the librarian. She might be able to help us."

Beau said, "Are you kidding? She has to be sixty years old and has a face like a jack-ass."

"Turn on the charm; she might have a key, or value her life enough to lead us out of here. A 60-year old broad could make a pretty effective hostage," Wendel pointed out.

Abbigail Pettigrew, the head librarian, was a spinster. Having noticed the pass key that she wore on a lanyard around her neck, with each day that passed, Beau did his best to work his magic on the old gal. Applying his good-natured charm and behaving like a choir boy, he did everything she asked, carefully, promptly, and with enthusiasm, eventually sitting side-by-side with her at the desk and doing his best to be endearing. His whole intent was to maintain unlimited access to the internet and gather up sufficient glue to keep the plan on track. He'd already snatched a pair of scissors. All he needed was that key.

After sharing his life story, how his father needed him to make and sell drugs and how his fiancée had been killed by a drug-crazed TV sports reporter, Ms. Abigail Pettigrew cracked, putting her arm around Beau to comfort him and giving him a motherly kiss on the cheek. "Boy, was he good," he thought to himself.

As the black plastic and rubber cement accumulated, the three firefighter coats and pants began to take shape. They also figured out that, using Ms. Pettigrew's passkey, they could open the utility closet in the library and set the fire there. Even better, Beau's unlimited computer searches led him to three compatriots in crime: In the Saginaw Correctional Institution, Milt Hofsteder had hooked up with Craig Raft and Jack Cannon. They all had, at one time, lived in Mesabi County and felt safer if they hung together as they moved about the prison. In addition, they had all been convicted thanks to the same team of individuals, led by the former Mesabi County Sheriff, Bill Bennett, and were feeling the same need for revenge. They, too, were seeking a way out of the hellhole, but couldn't come up with a way to get through the fencing – all around the perimeter of the prison was a double, 12-foot fence, topped with razor-ribbon wire with an electronic detection system on both the inner and outer fences. To make matters worse, there was a third fence even farther out, with its own electronic detection system, security cameras, and two gun towers where armed personnel were on patrol 24 hours a day.

Chapter Four

In addition to being assigned to getting scissors and rubber cement as well as getting into the library electrical closet, Beau was also responsible for handling the get-away vehicle. Scrolling down the list of EMTs within shooting distance of the prison, he came across a first responder by the name of Zabinski, There was an inmate by the name of Jerry Zabinski. How many Zabinskis could there be? Could he be related to Ed Zabinski? He would have to find out.

Using Pettigrew's password, Beau Wylie accessed the internet, and confirmed that Ed Zabinski was Jerry's father. He wrote the father's phone number down, and then planned what he would say, knowing that every conversation was monitored and recorded. He had to wait a day to be allowed the use of a telephone in the prison communication room. When a phone became available, he took the receiver and dialed.

"Hello," the voice said.

Beau Wylie said, "Hello, Ed. My name is Beau Wylie. I am a friend of your son Jerry's. He's really not feeling well, and he asked me to call you to see if you could come by the prison tomorrow during visiting hours."

Ed Zabinski said, "Not feeling well? I'll be there, visiting hours start at 8:30 a.m., right?" Beau Wylie had his name placed on the prisoner's visitor list the next day.

The next morning, Beau entered the visitors' room and settled into a chair, waiting for Zabinski. He saw an older man enter and take a seat across from him. They stared at each other through the Plexiglas, and then picked up the phones.

"How come Jerry never mentioned you before and that it's so important it couldn't wait for Jerry to tell me in person?" Ed

Zabinski demanded.

"Never mind, old man. You used to drive the city ambulance, right? Ed Zabinski said, "Yeah, so what?"

Beau continued, "You love your son and want him to be safe in here?"

"What are you getting at?" Ed Zabinski responded.

"If you don't cooperate, he's going to have a very bad accident. Do you understand?"

Ed Zabinski asked, "What do you want?"

Beau said, "There's going to be a fire at the prison. You just make sure that you're driving the ambulance next Tuesday. You drive right up to the emergency entrance and leave the ambulance unlocked with the keys in it. If you tell the screws, your son is dead. You understand?"

Zabinski nodded. Beau stood up, turned and walked out without another word.

Continuing to search the internet using Pettigrew's password, Beau reconnected with Tom McCann. McCann had been involved in a blackmail scheme; although, he was never formally charged, or imprisoned, he held Bennett responsible and was more than happy to assist them once they escaped. They agreed to meet in the Walmart parking lot, blocks from the prison, McCann would provide a get-away vehicle, and then join them in the trip north to get their revenge.

During the daily update, Fender said that he had heard that the head screw, Director Samuels of the Bureau of Prisons, was coming for a public relations visit the following Tuesday. Security would be high, but the panic level when a fire broke out in the library would be even higher. Luck was on their side at last.

Wendel ticked off the list of things they needed, stopping when he got to the wrench and a pair of wire cutters. "Either of you know someone in the machine shop?" he asked.

"I can get 'em," Fender replied.

Beau said that he would e-mail Ed Zabinski to remind him where to leave the ambulance and also send a message to

McCann confirming the rendezvous in the Walmart parking lot about 1:30."

He added, "And you know, I've had free access to the bitch's computer. The guys up in Saginaw ... Raft, Cannon and Hofsteder? They were screwed by those old codgers up north and are totally ready for revenge. They really want a piece of Bennett. They know the date and time of our escape, although they have to make their own exit plan. If they can get out, they'll meet us out front.

Wendel Wylie said, "They sound like my kind of guys."

Chapter Five

Milt Hofsteder was finally able to get access to a prison computer and read Beau Wylie's update. They only had three hours to make preparations.

He hurried to the prison yard. "What's up?" Raft asked.

"Tomorrow afternoon the Wylies and Fender are breaking out. If we're outside, they will pick us up," Hofsteder said.

Raft agreed, "I guess it's now, or never."

Hofsteder said, "I'll get us on the yard detail."

To protect their precious firemen's uniforms during the clean-up and inspection prior to the official visit from the Director of Prisons, Beau had started moving them a piece at a time into the library storage closet by wearing them under his uniform.

The big day arrived. The Wylies and Larry Fender were ready as the media inundated the prison. At 10:00 a.m., the inmates were ushered into the gymnasium, where Warden Caldwell offered a long diatribe outlining the wonderful improvements inside the prison since he became warden. The inmates didn't seem to appreciate the warden's efforts since most of them were excluded from the programs anyway. Then, the Director of Prisons was introduced, to minimal applause, and proceeded to tout his accomplishments, pointing out that the quality of life behind bars had improved under his guidance. In concluding his speech, he noted improvements to the library and other educational facilities and noted that he was headed there next. Any inmate who wanted their photos taken with him could join him there. He waited for applause, but there was none: members of the EME were totally occupied sending menacing glances, engaging in stare-downs, and making threatening gestures to the members of the AB, which were returned in kind.

On their way out, Beau Wylie whispered, "I can't believe our good luck. He is actually coming to the library."

"It's our lucky day, son," Wendel replied with a smile.

They trooped up to the library, Beau in the lead — he was the model prisoner and Ms. Pettigrew's right hand man, after all – with Wendel Wylie and Larry Fender following close behind. After shaking Ms. Pettigrew's hand, the director stood proudly to the side as one inmate after another lined up for a photo op that they really didn't want –doing so was just a way to obtain more time in the yard.   After 20 minutes had passed and things seemed to be going smoothly, Beau asked Ms. Pettigrew if he could use the employee's bathroom. He said, "He didn't want to miss a minute of the celebration and it would take too long to get out to the prisoners' bathrooms at the other end of the education wing." She hesitated for a minute, looked around at the heavy security, and handed him her pass key. "Thank you, Abby," he said, an angelic smile on his face.

While the guards watched the director and the long line of inmates who were waiting for a photo, Beau Wylie signaled to Wendel and Fender to join him. A few minutes apart, they slipped into the storage room and put on the firemen's uniforms under their prison clothing. Nonchalantly chatting with prisoners who were still in line, one at a time they disappeared around the corner toward the employee bathroom, where Fender took a wrench from his pocket, swung it at the conduit, which easily came loose from the wall, and cut the electrical wires. Sparks began to fly. They slipped out of the bathroom, propping the door open so as to disperse the smoke as quickly as possible, and rejoined the crowd. As smoke began to spew into the hallway, Beau Wylie shouted *"Fire!"*

Taking the disruption as a sign, members of *La Eme* began attacking members of the AB. The prison guards and state police didn't know where to turn first. The guards and state police quickly ushered the Director out of the library as smoke filled the corridor. The inmates who were locked in their cells called for help. Guards opened the cell doors and ordered the inmates to move to the prison yard. Before joining the crowd exiting the library, Beau grabbed Ms. Pettigrew's purse and removed her cash, credit cards, and cell phone. As she approached him Beau hit her in the temple with the wrench, and then quickly dragged her behind a bookcase.

They could hear the emergency vehicles approaching and knew that their moment had come. Ducking into a classroom just down the hall from the library, they stripped off their prison garb, revealing the firemen's uniforms. As trained firemen rushed toward the library Beau, Wendel and Larry intermingled with them. Entering the library, Beau went straight to the bookcase, picked up Ms. Pettigrew, and carried her down the stairs. Wendel Wylie and Larry Fender followed. No one challenged them as they walked out of the cell block and into the prison yard. Beau Wylie knelt over Pettigrew, acting like he was trying to revive her, giving her CPR for dramatic effect

Ed Zabinski drove the ambulance up to the emergency entrance. He and his partner immediately ran to assist Beau. Wendel and Larry Fender ducked into the cab of the ambulance. Beau Wylie stood up, pretending to be exhausted, and exchanged looks with Ed Zabinski. The paramedics knelt over Pettigrew as Beau Wylie slowly stepped backward, opened the back door and stepped into the ambulance. Larry put the ambulance in gear and roared toward the gate.

Wendel ordered, "Siren and lights." Larry Fender flipped them on and accelerated. The gate opened, and they sped out.

Beau shouted, "We're free,"

They drove until they reached the exit for Walmart. They pulled into the lot. With the lights flashing, customers turned and stared, but stayed back.

'We need to dump this ambulance and hook up with Tom McCann. Beau! Get inside, and steal some clothes," Wendel Wylie said.

They parked in front. Beau Wylie jumped out the back door and raced through the store. He grabbed three shirts and three pair of pants, then tucked them under his fireman's jacket and ran out the front door. No one challenged him.

In the Walmart parking lot, McCann reached in through the open window of an SUV that had just pulled into a parking space, threatened the woman driving the vehicle within an inch of her life, brandishing a revolver, pulled open the door, tossed her out onto the pavement, and raced over to the ambulance. Wylie and Fender jumped into the back seat of the stolen vehicle. When Beau ran out of Walmart, he dived inside next to McCann and they roared out of the lot, heading toward the highway.

Wendel asked Beau, "Do you know where to go? Give the directions to McCann as he drives."

"It's a no brainer. U.S. 23 past Ann Arbor to I-75." Beau Wylie boasted, "I took Pettigrew's cash, credit cards and her cell phone. We can get gas at convenience stores along the way. We should have no problem making it to Saginaw and on to Victorious."

They all smiled at the thought of what they were going to do when they got their hands on Bennett and his buddies.

Chapter Six

"This is a special bulletin" CNN announced. "There has been a prison escape at the Milan Federal Prison. Three inmates – Wendel Wylie, Beau Wylie, and Larry Fender – escaped by posing as emergency personnel during a fire. They later stole a black 2014 Buick Enclave. They are presumed armed and dangerous Do not try to apprehend them. Call your local law enforcement agency."

My phone rang. "Did you see what just aired on the news?" John Baldwin asked.

"Yeah." I said. "They are either running away from us or running toward us. We should be ready. See you at *Geno's Pizzeria* in one hour. I'll call Mark and Ben. You call Tyler."

Rick Bonnetelli brought over two pitchers of beer and said, "This is on the house as a small token of my appreciation of what you guys have done."

After settling into the booth, Mark said: "There's nothing the police can do until they've located the escapees. We'll have to be ready."

"They will probably come after you first," Ben said looking at me.

I said, "I'm sure they will."

Tyler asked, "So what's our plan?"

I said, "Let's set a trap of our own. I will be at my cottage with Barb, waiting in plain sight. The rest of you hide in the bedrooms. It takes about seven hours if they drive straight here. We have plenty of time to get ready."

"That sounds like a good plan to me," Mark said.

We loaded up on necessities at Jim's Jubilee, the local grocery store, and headed out to the cottage. They left their cars near at the point where South Camp Road separates from County Road 573. We drove to my cottage, commenting that it felt weird to be the hunted and not the other way around.

Later that afternoon, at the Saginaw Correctional Facility, the three inmates grabbed their rakes and proceeded to the front gate.

Milt Hofsteder said, "Remember. Beau Wylie said we had to be out front in the late afternoon, or they would leave us behind."

Jack Cannon asked, "What about the guards?"

"We take our chances," Raft said,

"We're taking a big chance," Jack Cannon said.

Craig Raft lost his patience. "Either you're in, or you're not. Make up your mind. I'm not going to hold your hand."

"I guess I'm in," Cannon said, as they took their rakes out of the supply shack and walked toward the front gate. They walked through the entrance and motioned to the second guard tower; the gate opened to bright sunshine and possible freedom, although they knew that the guards had them in their sights and would shoot them if they tried to make a run for it.

After driving through heavy traffic, Beau Wylie said, "Swing onto I-675. It will take us right to the Saginaw Correctional Facility. We'll drive by to see if those three yard birds are waiting."

Seeing the SUV as it slowed to a crawl in front of the prison, Raft, Cannon and Hofsteder dropped their rakes and ran. As predicted, the guards started firing, Cannon fell dead. Raft and Hofsteder zigged and zagged, then dove into the back of the vehicle and were whisked away. The prison siren sounded immediately, but served no purpose.

Beau Wylie said, "I was going to kill that guy anyway. The guards saved me the trouble."

They were making good time on I-75, but they needed to switch vehicles. "The state police will be looking for this one by now," Wendel Wylie said. The escapees, along with their accomplice Tom McCann stopped in Gaylord, checking the fast food parking lots for a vehicle they could steal. Beau found an old white Cadillac with the keys in the ignition. They pulled up next to it, switched vehicles and slowly drove away. Fearing that they'd be caught by the authorities when the crossed Big Mac, the bridge that connected the Superior Peninsula with Lower Michigan, they approached the toll booth with caution. When the ticket booth agent took the fee and raised the toll gate, they all breathed a sigh of relief. They continued on their way, taking U.S.-2 through Nottingham. The last time they were on this highway they were in a prison van. Now the shoe was on the other foot.

Wendel Wylie looked at McCann and asked, "Tell me again why you hate Bennett."

McCann pointed toward Hofsteder and said, "I was blackmailing this guy. This bum was sleeping with my wife. He raped and killed her and I was going to make him pay. Bennett got involved and fouled the whole thing up. I could have made enough money to live easy for a few years," Tom McCann said.

Hofsteder took a swing at McCann, but Wendel Wylie stopped him. "I told you, you cause trouble I won't hesitate to kill you."

"Okay, what about you, Raft?" Wendel Wylie asked.

"I helped another guy try to kill my wife. I would have gotten a fortune in the insurance settlement, but Bennett and his crew got involved and ruined it.

They drove north on a hilly road through the forest and past the nature preserve, then made a left unto M-28. Driving faster than the speed limit allowed, they were sure to attract police attention. Seeing flashing lights behind them, they pulled over. Raft and McCann got out of the car purportedly to relieve themselves, and then assaulted the police office from behind as she approached their car. Knocking her out, they grabbed her weapon, then dragged her body over into the marshy ditch along the side of the road. Problem solved.

Chapter Seven

"Where are we gonna find Bennett?" Wendel asked.

"He and his wife spend a lot of time at their cottage on the Dead River," Beau replied. "I'm guessing that's where we'll take them down."

"We have to be careful, though. They must know we'll be coming after them," Raft pointed out.

As they neared the cottage, they pulled over to the side and sent Hofsteder to check out the cottage. Up until now, he'd contributed little to the plan so far. He returned half an hour later. "The deputy posted in front won't be a problem anymore," he reported.

Once the cottage was in sight, they piled out of the car and put their plan into action.

Chapter Eight

I was passing time in the kitchen trying to stay busy while Barb relaxed in the Lazy-Boy in the adjoining living room. I could hear Mark Kestila snoring in the back bedroom. No doubt he would be well rested when we needed him. Ben and John were lounging in the second bedroom. We had the lights turned down and the television was on. Everything was to appear to be as normal as possible. I sat at the kitchen table, pretending to work a crossword puzzle. I was trying to keep my mind occupied, but it wasn't working.

I heard a rustling in the small entrance way off the kitchen and suddenly I couldn't breathe. My mouth was covered with a rag doused in something that made me feel nauseous. I struggled. "If you move, I will kill you and your wife, too," Wendel Wylie said. He put a pistol to my head.

I raised my arms to show that I was not resisting. I watched helplessly as they struck Barb in the back of the head, and then held a kitchen knife to her throat. Wendel Wylie found a piece of rope in a drawer and tied her hands behind her back, then secured mine, too.

"What do you want? The police are out front. Get out now," Barb threatened.

"Your deputy friend isn't going to be helping anybody ever again." Beau chuckled."

"What are you going to do with me?" Barb asked.

"We're going to put on a show for your husband and you're going to be the star attraction," Wendel Wylie retorted.

In the meantime, the other escapees had cased the back bedrooms. Although Mark woke up when he heard brawling in the other room, he arrived too late to be any help and merely

succeeded in getting himself bound too. The convicts marched
a sorry-looking trio – Mark, Ben, and John – out into the living
room. It was one un-happy reunion for us.

"How could we be so stupid?" exclaimed Ben.

"Shut up," Beau Wylie threatened. "I'm going to have the
time of my life cutting you up. But first you get to watch this
bitch get slaughtered," Wendel Wylie shouted.

He opened several kitchen drawers until he found a fillet knife.
"Guess what? We're going to have a carving party. I want it to be
slow. Let's take our time and enjoy it," Wendel said gleaming.

"Who wants to go first?" Beau asked.

"How about me?" A thunderous voice bellowed.

I knew that voice, but couldn't remember whose it was. Then
it came to me and I smiled.

John Crane stepped through the door. He knocked Larry Fender
right through the front window. When Beau Wylie charged the
Man-mountain bent down, throwing Beau over his shoulder like
a rag. When Wendel Wylie ran toward him with the fillet knife,
Crane sidestepped him, hitting him hard enough to render him
unconscious before he even hit the kitchen floor. Craig Raft
threw a hay-maker, but Crane stopped the swing, grabbed him
by the throat and squeezed, breaking his neck. He threw Raft's
lifeless body against the wall. Hofsteder grabbed the fillet knife
out of Wendel's hand and charged him. John Crane was ready.
He dodged the knife, then grabbed Hofsteder and snapped his
neck.

Beau got to his feet and charged again, but the Man-Mountain
hit him flush on the chin, breaking his jaw instantly. Beau Wylie
howled in pain. Larry Fender was back; he staggered through
the door with an axe and threw it wildly end-over-end at Crane.
Man-Mountain grabbed the axe in mid-air and returned the favor.
The blade struck Fender square in the back. He screamed, and
then fell to the floor. Wendel Wiley was back in the game, but
John Crane walked over to him, kicked him in the ribs, and said
in a un-sympathetic tone, "I bet that hurts." Then Man-Mountain
smashed his head on the floor. Wendel Wylie didn't move as he

drew his last breath.

John Crane looked at the five of us. "Boys, you are one sorry lot, not to mention stupid! You let this ragtag outfit sneak up on you. And to think what you put your wife through. This could have ended very, very badly for you amateur detectives," Crane said.

"How in the hell did you know where to find us?" I asked.

"I figured that when these idiots broke out, they'd come for you. I just followed you and the other old geezers out to the cottage. Then I waited in the shadows until you were all assembled in the same room. From there, it was easy pickings. And by the way, there's a hundred thousand dollar reward for each of these yard birds. Wire the reward to my off-shore bank right?" he said, "And no big stories about this in the news. I was never here."

"No problem. You saved our lives and I owe you," I said.

With that, he turned, walked out the front door.

"Aren't you going to untie us?" I called after him, but he had already disappeared into the night. We'd have to handle that on our own. With the fillet knife clutched awkwardly in my hands, I managed to slowly cut through the rope around Mark's hands, and then he freed the rest of us. We called Tyler, and then the police.

Tyler arrived first. "What happened?" Tyler asked in amazement.

"You wouldn't believe me if I told you," I said. Knowing that at least Tyler deserved to know the truth, I said, "Believe it or not, Man-Mountain was here; he saved the day. Otherwise, somebody else would have found us in a sea of blood on the cottage floor."

Sheriff Remington arrived hot on Tyler's heels. "I'm guessing you had some help," he stated, looking quizzically from one of us to the others. When we didn't respond, he continued: "I can't approve of your methods, but your friend sure has his own way of controlling crime."

We heard sirens in the distance. The sheriff and his team would take it from here. Barb and I embraced, then we followed our friends out the door. No one was going to be staying here for a few days, that was for sure.

We did appreciate the unsigned Christmas card that was postmarked from the Cayman Islands every year. Good friends are hard to find. We wouldn't soon forget the *Revenge on the Dead River*.

Bibliography

Dunbar, Willis Frederick, *Michigan: A History of the Wolverine State,* William B. Eerdman Publishing Company, Grand Rapids, 1965

"How to Fly a Helicopter: 8 Steps WikiHow." Wikipedia: *The Free Encyclopedia. Wikimedia Foundation, Inc. January 11, 2016. Web. January 6, 2016. (<http: //en.wikipedia.org/wiki/ how to fly a helicopter>)*

LaFayette, Kenneth D. *The Way of the Pine Forest Industries of Marquette County during the white pine era 1848-1912. LaFayette.* 2008

FCI Milan. Federal Bureau of Prisons , Retrieved June 3, 2016 (http ://www.fcimilanfederalprisonfacility)

Saginaw Correctional Facility Official Site, Retrieved March 22, 2016. (http://www.saginawcorrectionalfacility)